Stealing Forever

Written
by
Susan Wells Bennett

Published by
Inknbeans Press
©2015

Cover by Nikki McBroom
© 2015 Susan Wells Bennett and Inknbeans Press

ISBN-13: 978-0692452790 (Inknbeans Press)

ISBN-10: 0692452796

Contents

Chapter 1 San Diego, California -- 2105

Evelyn pressed her finger against the big green "GO" button and looked directly at the illuminated crosshairs on her rear-view mirror, hoping against hope that the reason her hovercraft didn't start was because it hadn't gotten a good scan of her eye. The almost-new, hot pink vehicle clicked loudly, but didn't get off the ground. It was definitely dead.

She dropped her head against the front dash in disgust and frustration. First the diagnosis -- her cancer was back again -- and now this. Nothing about this day was going the way she planned.

She swiveled to look when someone tapped on her window and motioned for her to roll it down. She almost laughed at the oddity of the twenty-something on the outside of the glass rotating her hand -- Evelyn knew, without a doubt, that the girl had never even seen a hand-cranked window. Even she hadn't seen one in decades. Unable to comply, she pressed the button that raised the door.

"Are you aware that your meter has expired?" the young woman asked, pointing with her laser pen at the device on the other side of her hovercraft. With her free hand, she pulled her ticketing device from its holster on her hip.

"I'm sorry, officer," Evelyn purred -- one never knew when one's sexual appeal might be a benefit these days. "My vehicle won't start."

"Have you called for a tow?"

"I only just realized the problem."

The girl glanced at the meter. "The time expired more than ten minutes ago."

Evelyn looked at her watch: 13:13. Shit. Of course. "I've been here longer than I realized," she said dully. She glanced in the mirror, where she saw to her horror that her eyes were puffy and a crease had formed in the center of her forehead. "I just came from the clinic. I had some bad news."

"You're still in one piece -- it can't have been that bad." The officer began tapping on her device, intent on giving her a ticket.

"Do you know who I am?" Evelyn asked, moving to her argument of last resort.

"I really don't care, ma'am," she answered, not even looking up. "Look -- just chalk this up to a bad day. You live long enough, you have plenty of them."

Evelyn's eyes cut sharply back to the officer, taking in details she hadn't noticed before. The girl had a platinum wedding ring on her finger and no visible tattoos -- not even the ones all new cops got on their wrists and ankles. This woman was old. Maybe not old enough to remember hand-cranked windows, but certainly older than the twenty-something she appeared to be. "I don't have ten people who care whether I live or die."

The officer paused, lifting her stylus from the device. "But you're Evelyn Bryant."

"Yes, I am."

"I watch you on the news all the time."

"Not lately you haven't. I was fired three years ago."

The woman shook her head. "No way. I know I just saw you--"

"Wasn't me," she interjected. "My salary was getting too high -- too many years in the chair. The producers did a good job of recasting though, didn't they?"

The officer cast a disgusted look at the ticket she was writing and hit the delete button. "Listen," she said, "I don't usually do this. You have to develop a thick skin working around here, you know?"

"Yeah," Evelyn answered. "Thanks. I'll get a tow right away."

The cop paused and pulled off her sunglasses, revealing blue eyes that held the knowledge of a long life. "You really don't have ten people?"

She shook her head. "I just had a dose of the Cure a few years ago. I had to buy one affidavit."

"Shh!" The officer glared at her. "You should know better."

Fear sprang to Evelyn's eyes.

"Don't worry. Age has its perks. No one's reviewing my tapes these days unless I'm involved in a stunning incident." She patted her sidearm and smiled. "I haven't had to use the stunner in quite a while. But you need to be more careful about what you say. Do you have your affidavit collector with you?"

Of course she did. The clinic had just given her a new one to go along with the diagnosis. She had heard the stories -- everyone had -- about strangers who would still give away their affidavits out of the kindness of their hearts. Not that she expected to meet any of those strangers. But she could hope. She opened the vehicle's center console and held it up. "Don't leave home without it," she said, echoing a commercial from her youth.

"Hand it over," the officer said.

Reluctantly, Evelyn gave the woman the device. Pressing the "collect" button, the officer said, "My name is Marta Gamble. Evelyn Bryant deserves to live."

The device vibrated in her hand and an electronic voice answered, "Thank you, Marta Gamble. Please look directly at the crosshairs on the screen. Do not blink." Officer Gamble stared at the device for a few seconds until it vibrated again. "Marta Gamble, please provide your DNA sample."

"I hate this part," the woman said, shuddering. She slid her finger over the small hole at the top of the device. A second later, she winced and stuck her finger in her mouth.

"Affidavit collected," the machine said. "Nine more affidavits required."

Marta -- Evelyn felt they were on a first-name basis now -- handed the collector back to her.

"You shouldn't have done that," Evelyn said, shaking her head in disbelief.

"Why not?"

"I'm a stranger -- just someone you met on the street. What if you need that affidavit for someone you love?"

Marta waved her hand as though the thought were no more than a gnat. "I have a huge family, Evelyn. We take care of each other. Besides, you are a friend to me -- we have coffee together every morning." She shrugged. "At least...we used to. I can't believe that's not you. The network still uses your name."

"It's trademarked. I let them have it as part of contract negotiations about ten years ago."

"I'm surprised they don't sue you for continuing to use it."

"I was 'grandfathered' in. One of the few good negotiations I ever made on my own behalf."

Marta shook her head. "Good thinking." She shoved her ticketing device into her back pocket and replaced her sunglasses. "Have a good day, ma'am," the officer said, walking away.

Evelyn pressed the "service" button and waited for her tow to show up.

Chapter 2 Oregon -- 2045

"It's your only chance, Evie," Carmen had said.

"It's an experiment!" Evie remembered exclaiming. Her older sister was a physician: Dr. Carmen Mendoza. She trusted medicine more than her own family -- and, in 2045, she wanted Evie to be a medical pincushion. "I've had a good life. Maybe it's just my time to go."

"You're only fifty-five. I know you're still sad about Marty, but he wouldn't have wanted you to follow him into an early grave."

Just the sound of his name made her gasp as if an asthma attack were coming on. Deep breaths, she chanted to herself. Deep, soothing breaths. When she felt in control, she answered, "You're right. I miss Marty, and I miss the life we shared. But it's not like I'm refusing to eat. I have cancer, Carmen. It's in my organs -- my liver, my pancreas. I might as well spend what's left of Marty's money on a cruise around the world."

"The cancer you have is aggressive and it will kill you, so what have you got to lose?"

"What if this medical trial makes my last few months miserable? Right now, I feel fine -- at least, most of the time I do."

Carmen sighed and leaned her head against her youngest sister's shoulder. "Please, Evie. You're all the family I have left. Don't go without a fight."

Evie caressed her sister's gray hair and agreed to try. After all, Carmen was right: who else did either of them have?

The clinical trial turned out to be fairly painless as these things go: just a quick injection and a pat on the back. She had a one-in-three chance of receiving the new drug, which was called Promorterem. One-third of the patients received a shot of chemo, and the final third received the equivalent of a sugar pill injected into their bloodstream. Of the three options, only the chemo was supposed to cause any immediate side effects. However, as the sister and widow of doctors, she assumed she received the placebo when she didn't have any reaction at all to the injection.

Carmen, on the other hand, held out hope that her sister would soon recover. She checked on Evie every morning before she left for work from the day of the injection forward. "How are you feeling?"

"Same as before," Evie answered mirthlessly on the fourth day. "Like I'm dying. How are you?"

Carmen sighed dramatically. "How many times have I told you that a positive attitude is more than half the cure?"

"I'm sorry...it's hard to be positive when I know I'm stuffed full of disease."

She frowned and rolled her eyes -- an expression Evie had seen her sister use to express doubt and frustration with her naivete. Evelyn found it ironic that it was now so closely associated with her sister's optimism. "Are you hungry? I'll fix you some breakfast."

"Not really."

"You've got to eat something," Carmen urged. "How about some cereal?"

Evie shook her head. "A slice of toast, maybe. With jam."

Her sister disappeared and Evie fell back against her pillow. She had never been a natural early riser. Now her sister was determined to make the last months of her life miserable by forcing her to not only wake up before eight in the morning, but also to eat breakfast. Her eyes were aching in their sockets -- not horribly, but enough for her to think a painkiller might be in order. She rolled to her side and tugged open the bedside table's drawer, digging around in it until she came up with a bottle of aspirin. For the first time in thirty-five years, she wished for a hit of heroin. Now that was a painkiller, she chuckled to herself. That shit would make everything go away -- the cancer, this headache, her sister -- at least for a little while.

Resigned, she rolled onto her back and scanned the label for the maximum dosage. Two pills. She opened the bottle and shook them out, replacing the cap with her empty hand and dropping the container back in the drawer. Reaching over blindly, she located her water and propped herself up on one elbow to swallow the pills. Setting the glass back on the nightstand and allowing herself to fall back onto the pillow, she reached up to remove her glasses.

She didn't have them on.

Her mind raced backwards, searching for the moment when she had taken them off. She hadn't. Perhaps she had simply remembered that the dosage was two pills? She reached into the drawer, attempting to retrieve the container. Instead, her fingers closed on a small bottle of lotion. She held it in front of her and found that she could easily read the advertising copy on the back of it. She felt her face again for her glasses -- they were definitely not there. She hadn't been able to read fine print without them since she was forty-six.

She sat up quickly, then stood up. No dizziness accompanied her rapid change of elevation. She launched herself toward the mirror at the far end of the room. Standing just inches from it, she studied her face. She lifted her gown and checked the inside of her thighs, where the skin had begun to sag in the last few years. Not only did the skin look tighter, it felt thicker than it had in decades.

She closed her eyes and shook her head quickly, attempting to clear it of the illusions now taunting her. She wondered if chemo ever caused hallucinations.

"What are you doing?" Carmen asked as she walked back into the room with the small plate holding Evie's breakfast.

"I think," Evie answered softly, "that I'm losing my mind."

Carmen slid the plate onto her nightstand and walked over to stand behind her. Carmen had always been taller than she; as they aged, they seemed to shrink at nearly the same rate. Now, though, they could both plainly see that they were almost the same height -- Carmen was less than an inch taller. Carmen blinked. "What--? I don't understand." She stepped away from Evie and looked at her sister's feet. "You're not wearing shoes."

Evie pointed out the obvious: "You are."

Carmen's face lit up and tears sprang to her eyes. "You got the cure!"

#

Promorterem, better known as the Cure, was the pet project of a tech billionaire named Mose Baxter. Baxter believed that immortality was within the grasp of humanity, if only humanity had the good sense to pool their knowledge. In his estimation, the false dividers between different fields of study were hindering progress. To prove it, he funded a research center dedicated to creating the cure for death.

Carmen had heard whispers about it for years. That's how it was in the medical community: rumors of future drugs made the rounds, always as second-, third-, or even fourth-hand information. Most of them fizzled before they ever made it to clinical trials. The wonder drug that could cure pancreatitis with one pill led to kidney failure in ninety out of the hundred mice drafted for the study. The cure for herpes caused sterility. And a drug that was supposed to improve cognition in dementia patients made the chimps treated with it violent.

But the whispers around Promorterem were different. It wasn't a drug, per se -- it was a biological computer program. And it wasn't meant to treat a single physical ailment. No -- this "drug" treated all of them. It eradicated cancer, restored pancreatic function, even rebuilt the brain.

There were a few unexpected complications once the drug made it to human trials. The Cure erased tattoos, closed piercings, and caused previous surgical alterations to one's body to disappear. One of the women in a separate trial awoke to find her nose had grown and her breasts had deflated overnight. However, even such unexpected consequences were soon forgotten. The only thing that really mattered was that she wasn't going to die of multiple sclerosis.

Patients who had already undergone transplant surgeries were quickly deemed unsuitable -- particularly those with foreign hearts. Promorterem couldn't be altered to build a new organ before destroying the "enemy" organ. Therefore, those patients were, in her sister's words, "as good as dead."

Mose Baxter was a reclusive philanthropist who wanted to save the world. When the drug was finally approved -- several years after Evelyn participated in the trial that saved her life -- he created the Fountain of Life Foundation (or FOLF, as it is known). Baxter gave the formula for creating Promorterem and all but a billion dollars of his fortune to FOLF, stipulating that the "drug" must never be available for cash. FOLF decided that all doses would require ten affidavits -- sworn statements from individuals who believed a person deserved to live.

Initially, everyone was allowed to give ten affidavits each year. In other words, if you were liked by ten people, chances were good that you would easily gather ten affidavits. Even if you didn't know ten people who liked you, the black market was flooded with affidavits for sale, since most people believed that the chance of ten people they knew and loved personally all becoming terminally ill within the same twelve months was, at worst, unlikely. A hermit with access to a computer terminal could easily seek out and gather ten affidavits for a hundred dollars, more or less. If a person happened to get their diagnosis in late November, they could stand on the corner with a sign and easily get ten strangers to give them their affidavits for free, since they expired on December 31st of each year.

After a few years of this, the foundation began to tighten the noose, so to speak. They were looking for the perfect number of affidavits to afford each person -- the number that would produce something close to zero population growth. They dropped the number to eight; the black market price increased to a hundred dollars per affidavit. When they dropped the number to six, the price rose to two-hundred-and-fifty bucks. When they changed the system so that the affidavits were allotted on a rolling basis rather than an annual one, the price rose again: $350 became the lowest price. Over the course of three years in the latter half of the 2070s, they dropped the number of affidavits a person could give to just three. The black market dried up; very few people were comfortable with surrendering a single affidavit, no matter how much money they received in exchange. People finally saw that the only real way to secure a dose of the Cure was to be a kind, decent, and friendly human being.

The billionaire, however, had never overcome his own reclusive nature. His beloved wife, Maharene, was the only one at his bedside when he died.

#

Three weeks after receiving her dose of the Cure, the roots of Evelyn's hair were the deep chestnut brown she had been born with, making her look like a photo negative come to life. She wrapped her head with a scarf before she would allow Carmen to drive her to the first of what would become two years' worth of follow-up appointments.

Carmen insisted on coming into the examination room with her. As they sat waiting, Carmen asked, "How does it feel?"

"Strange," Evelyn answered. "Every time I look in the mirror, I have to touch it just to be sure I'm not looking at an old photograph of myself. Even with the gray hair to remind me, my face just looks so..."

"Young?" Carmen supplied.

"I suppose that's it. But I don't remember looking like this when I was young."

"You didn't. You were already on the drugs before you reached full maturity. You went right from fresh and young to sunken cheeks and dark circles under your eyes."

"But I looked better after Alan helped me get clean, didn't I?"

She shrugged. "You were healthier. But once you lose the rosy glow of youth, it never comes back...at least, it never did before."

The doctor -- a woman more accustomed to working with Guinea pigs than humans -- entered the small room. "You're Cancer Number 111, right?" she asked, not bothering to look up from the datapad she was balancing against her hip with one hand.

Evelyn confirmed that she was correct.

"Excellent. How are you feeling?"

"Rejuvenated," she said, half smiling.

The doctor looked up from the board and nodded thoughtfully. "Let's get your vitals and then I'm going to send you for a full-body scan."

"She received the Cure, didn't she?" Carmen asked.

"I'm sorry...who are you?"

"I'm her sister."

11

"I'm sorry, ma'am, but you aren't allowed back here."

"It's all right -- I'm a physician."

The young woman frowned. "You still aren't supposed to be back here. This is a clinical trial and--"

"Look, sweetheart, I know your boss personally. Jacob Evans and I go way back."

The doctor straightened her spine and arched her brows at Carmen. "Good for you. I'm sure you must be aware that we aren't allowed to reveal who received what treatment until the clinical trial is complete."

"Oh, for God's sake," Evelyn muttered as she pulled off her scarf. Pointing at her head, she said, "I've never heard of this being a side effect of chemo or placebos."

The doctor walked closer and examined the roots of Evelyn's hair. She wrote a quick note on the datapad with her finger. When she made eye contact with Evelyn again, the doctor smirked. "Count your blessings. It could have fallen out."

For the longest time, Evelyn couldn't stop staring at her reflection. In her smooth skin and bright, young eyes, she saw a miracle she had never witnessed before. "Marty would have hated this," she whispered quietly to her reflection.

Marty, her doctor, the man who had healed her soul, would have been made obsolete by the "drug" that saved her life.

"What are you doing?" Carmen asked from the doorway.

"Just...you know...looking."

"It's been months, Evelyn. I think you've crossed over from wonder to vanity."

Evelyn glanced up sharply to see her sister smirking at her.

"Almost makes me wish I had a terminal illness," she mused. "I wasted my youth...wouldn't mind another shot at it."

"What good is youth when I'm alone?"

"Don't be so melodramatic! You're not alone. You have me. And I bet Desmond would love to see you."

"You know that's not what I mean." She put her hand against the young face in the mirror. "I miss Marty."

"Marty's been gone for five years, Evie."

"And I was supposed to be with him. If you had just left well enough alone..."

"You'd be dead!"

"Exactly."

Carmen's jaw dropped. "You...you wanted to die?"

Sitting down on the bed, she let her shoulders slump forward. "More than anything."

"Fine," Carmen said sharply. "I'll get you some pills. Or would you prefer a razor blade? A gun?"

"I can't kill myself," she mumbled.

"Why on earth not? If that's what you really want, just do it. Throw away this gift of a new life..."

"I already had a new life, thanks to Jesus Christ."

"Oh, please," she scoffed, "you don't still believe that crap, do you? Besides, doesn't He frown on divorcees?"

Evelyn narrowed her eyes. "Don't make fun of my beliefs, Carmen."

"I thought you left those behind when you walked out on Alan."

"It turns out some things are harder to leave behind than others."

Carmen sat down next to her. "Marty didn't believe in God."

"You're wrong about that. While we were on the Mercy ship, he started reading the Bible. He found God, Carmen. He's in Heaven, waiting for me."

"Oh, honey," Carmen said softly, "there's no such place."

Evie laughed and shook her head. "I have to believe there is. Otherwise, why should I go on?"

Chapter 3 Evie's Second Chance

"Name?" A bored college student asked from behind the counter.

"Evelyn Bryant."

"Bryant...Evelyn..." the kid said, scrolling through the antique registrar's computer. The thing even had a keyboard -- no one used a keyboard anymore. "Found you. Key in your Student ID here," he said, placing a numeric pad in front of her. She dutifully entered it.

The kid -- he was at least a decade younger than her youngest child -- smiled at her as if he had only just noticed she was attractive. "Say...did you know that there's a party at Alpha Eta Rho tonight?"

"No. I'm new. I just moved into my dorm room today."

"That's right. I see here you're a freshman. Welcome."

"Thank you. I just want to--"

"Don't worry," he said, taking her handwritten class schedule from her. "This will only take a few secs." He rapidly keyed in her class selections. "Are you planning to go into journalism?"

"Um...yes. How did you get that from--?"

"I've been doing this for a few years. Nothing gives it away faster than a beautiful woman with a schedule full of writing and speech classes."

Evelyn blushed. "Look, I just--"

"Wait right here. I'll get your schedule." As he walked away from her, she noted his muscular figure. He must have been involved in the sports program, though she couldn't imagine why a football player would be working in the registrar's office. One thing had remained constant throughout her life: football players earned their spots on campus with their bodies, not their minds. And they never paid a dime for their "education."

"Here you are, Evelyn Bryant," he said, sliding the paper across the counter to her. At the last moment he pulled it back and scribbled a phone number at the top of the page. "If you get bored in your dorm room tonight, give me a call."

"I thought there was a party."

"There is. But I'll skip it for you."

The guy behind her in line cleared his throat. She turned around just in time to see him roll his eyes and nudge a friend who was standing with him.

She took her schedule and headed toward the campus commons. She hadn't made any friends yet, and she wasn't sure she would be able to. When she decided to go to college, she hadn't considered how a college campus might feel to someone who had already lived a full life. Even that handsome young man looked like a child to her.

She wished she could go back in time -- not just be physically younger but mentally as well. If she could think like a teenaged girl, she would be able to be young and dumb. She could make all the stupid mistakes college kids make. When she was actually eighteen, college had been out of the question. Her parents had made a few unwise choices. The first was to allow Carmen to use most of the money they had saved for their children's educations to go to an Ivy League college. Okay -- so she was the most brilliant of their daughters and she did become a doctor. She could have done that at a state school, though, right? The second mistake was sending Karen to business school with the money from a second mortgage on their home. But it was

2003 and everyone was doing that. Home prices were soaring to astronomical heights and even her normally rational parents fell into the trap. By the time Evelyn was ready to start college in 2008, the college fund, such as it had been, was depleted. Her parents began squabbling about money nearly every night. When Evelyn asked for help in order to attend a state school, they told her she would have to work her way through college.

She bought a drink from a vending machine and found an empty table. A blonde she had met in her dorm that morning spotted her and waved. When Evelyn waved back, the girl took it as an invitation to join her.

"Evelyn, right?" the girl asked.

"Yeah," she answered, "and you're...Mary?"

"Close. Mayra. I've spent the last twenty years answering for my parents' creativity." She rolled her huge green eyes in an exaggerated manner. "Have you met your roomie yet?"

Evelyn had considered spending the extra money to get a single room, but ultimately decided having a roommate would be a better college experience. She was already regretting it. "No. Have you?"

She shrugged. "Who knows? I've been welcoming new students all morning."

"You're a junior, right?"

"Yeah."

"Do you think you're getting a good education for your money?"

Mayra shrugged and laughed. "Good enough, I guess. You must be taking loans, huh?" When Evelyn didn't immediately answer, she said, "It's nothing to be embarrassed about. Lots of students are here thanks to the government loan programs. My parents are paying for me though. That's what they get for being 'traditionalists.'"

"How do you mean?"

"You know -- they got jobs instead of trying to live off the grid." Mayra gave her a quick up-and-down glance with slightly narrowed eyes, as if she were trying to read some fine print on Evelyn's body. "Let me guess...I'm pretty good at this. Your parents are...artists. Real flighty types, I'm guessing. Maybe they're even part of one of those communes out west. No house, no personal property to speak of...I bet you grew up in one of those five-hundred-square-foot jobs where everything fits together like a puzzle. They probably said cheesy shit like 'Love grows best in small houses.' Am I right?"

Evelyn smiled noncommittally, suddenly understanding her own children a little better. Her son actually did live in one of those tiny homes when he wasn't traveling the world. Her daughter was homeschooling her daughter, though their home was considerably larger than 500 square feet. The only time she had visited -- not long after Marty's death -- her daughter had said something that struck her as cheesy: *the world is Abigail's classroom.*

"I knew it!" Mayra crowed. "I am so good, I scare myself! Then again, you have rebellion written all over you. That outfit screams twentieth-century schoolmarm. You must really hate them."

"I just...I'm very different from them."

"Keep telling yourself that, sweetie. I'm majoring in genetic studies, and I know for a fact that no one falls far from their family tree." The girl put on an air of knowledge that made Evelyn want to scoff. Somehow she managed to hold her tongue. "So, what's your major going to be?"

"Journalism."

Mayra nodded. "I can see that. You've got a trustworthy face. And not just that -- you're pretty too. Cameras love girls like you."

"I always loved Diane Sawyer," Evelyn said. "I wanted to be just like her when I grew up."

Her companion scrunched her face. "Who's that again?"

"She was a respected newswoman a few decades ago."

"Wow. So you, what? Researched her or something? 'Cause I've never even heard of her."

"I guess you could say that." She made a note to pick someone more contemporary as her role model.

"What does that mean? Was she your grandmother?"

"No. I just...you know, saw clips and thought she was great. Hard-hitting, honest, unafraid..."

"That's interesting," Mayra said in a way that made it clear she didn't really think it was.

Evelyn felt heat rise to her cheeks. "I guess I'm a nerd."

"A news nerd!" Mayra laughed. "That's all right...I'll help you get hip. You're too pretty to be relegated to the geek group."

Evelyn didn't know if she wanted Mayra's help, but she knew she couldn't afford to turn her down. She may have looked twenty-something, but she still thought like a nearly sixty-year-old woman, and the only way to mask that would be to learn to act young.

Her roommate turned out to be a mousy little girl whose parents had named Arleta. She was the fifth girl in a family holding out hope for an Arlo Junior who never came along. She certainly wasn't going to be much help in Evelyn's quest to become more like her new set of peers -- the poor thing had grown up in one of those communes that Mayra had assumed Evelyn was from. She was smaller than Evelyn, both in height and build. Her hair was an unfortunate shade that fell somewhere between blonde and brown. Though Arleta tried to hide it, Evelyn knew her family nickname was Mouse before the week was out -- the collection of stuffed animals and figurines was a dead giveaway. A less mature roommate might have used the name against her, but Evelyn took a more protective stance with Arleta.

Others in the dorm were quick to pounce on Arleta's weakness; they shunned her almost as if by instinct.

"You must be miserable," Mayra said one day as they walked together toward the Liberal Arts building.

"Why would you think that?" Evelyn asked, shifting her almost-weightless bag to her other shoulder. She wasn't even sure why she continued to carry a bag at all -- few of her fellow students did, opting instead to carry their lightweight computer tablets in their hands.

"I bet your roommate squeaks all night long." She giggled behind her hand.

Evelyn reddened. "Arleta is a sweet girl."

"I don't know why her family bothered to send her to school. She's just going to end up back at the commune."

"You don't know that. She's brilliant, you know. She plans to be a scientist of some sort."

"Probably a geologist," Mayra shrugged. "I bet she would be embarrassed to learn biology."

"I'm serious, Mayra! Stop picking on her."

"Geez! What, are you two from the same commune? Is she your sister?" Mayra stopped walking. "Oh, my God! She is, isn't she? You two are from one of those plural-marriage communes, right? You have the same mother!"

"Don't be ridiculous."

"Holy shit! I can't believe they let you freaks in!"

"Mayra, knock it off. I didn't know Arleta before we became roommates."

Her companion's face relaxed into a smirk. "Well, that's a relief. Now that we've established you don't know each other, you can stop protecting her like she's related to you."

They began walking again as Evelyn fumed silently.

"Hey, I'm sorry. I'm just teasing."

Evelyn chewed over her words for a few paces before nodding. "It's all right."

"I heard about a job opening at the local radio station," Mayra said cheerfully, changing the subject. "You should apply for it. It would be a great place to start!"

"Thanks. I'll do that."

# # #

A week later, as she walked to class with Mayra, her phone rang.

"Mom? Is that you?" The young woman's voice sounded remarkably like Evelyn's own. Her heart thumped so hard she thought it was trying to escape her chest. She sat down on the nearest bench and crossed her free arm over her chest.

Mayra, wearing an expression of annoyance imitating concern, stopped next to her. *Radio station?* she mouthed.

Evelyn shook her head no, and waved her away with her elbow.

Mayra shrugged and walked away slowly, looking back a few times with curiosity blazing through her eyes.

"Mom, are you there?"

"Just a moment," Evelyn answered as she waited for Mayra to get completely out of earshot.

"You sound different," Hope said. "Are you all right?"

Finally certain she wouldn't be overheard, Evelyn answered, "I'm fine. Perfect, in fact."

"Why didn't you tell me that you moved? I was so scared when I called your phone and it was disconnected. Aunt Carmen was no help at all -- she wouldn't tell me where you are! She only gave me this number because I begged..."

Evelyn tried to listen to her panicky daughter's monologue, but she found her thoughts drifting away from Hope's words. Carmen had tried to discuss this eventuality with her, but Evelyn had been certain her children would

21

never seek her out again. When her sister asked what she should say if Hope or Desmond called, Evelyn had glibly answered, "Tell them I died." After all, how would she explain her newfound youth to her children -- both of whom were in their thirties? She wished she had left without giving Carmen her new phone number, but she couldn't cut her sister off completely.

"Mom? Are you there?"

"Yes, Hope, I'm here."

"What's going on?" The slight whine in her voice made Evelyn cringe, just as it had back when she was raising the girl.

"Don't whine. It's unbecoming," she snapped. Evelyn's own mother had driven the annoying habit out of her with those words, but they never worked on Hope.

"Fine. I just called to let you know that Dad is sick. I think he's going to die."

"What do the doctors say?"

"It's his heart. It's not functioning right, and they say he's too old for a replacement organ." The insurance companies had made that rule: if you were over eighty, you might as well lay down and die if you got sick. The bloodsucking fiends wouldn't insure you for so much as a free aspirin. With Medicare a distant memory, many older couples made suicide pacts rather than spending every last dime they had just to stay alive. In fact, when she met her second husband, the majority of his medical practice had been in euthanasia. He used to tell her to squeeze every drop of life out while she was healthy, because most of his patients expressed regret for wasting their lives waiting for some great reward that never came.

"How long does he have?"

"A few weeks, at most." She hesitated. "Mom, he'd really like to see you. He keeps asking for you."

"He can't even remember me," Evelyn answered.

"He does...just an earlier version of you."

She laughed at the irony.

"This isn't funny. Damn it. You know what? Forget it. Forget I called. I can't believe I actually thought you would come. What was I thinking? After all, the man only saved your life and fathered your children--"

"I'll be there," Evelyn interrupted.

Her daughter paused. "Really?"

"Yes. But I should warn you--"

"Soon, right? This weekend would be best."

"Yes. I'll schedule a flight after--" she stopped herself from saying class. "This afternoon. I'll send you the schedule. But you need to know--"

"Good. Thanks, Mom. Desmond is flying in as well. I'll send you his travel plans via text. Could you try to schedule your flight for around the same time as his?"

"I'll do my best. Hope, you need to--"

"Sorry, gotta go. Glen's waiting for me."

Evelyn let her hand holding the phone drop to her lap. She stared across the green lawn of her college campus and sighed.

#

Evelyn first met Alan Shaw as he picketed outside of a porn superstore where she was signing autographs. As she teetered out on too-high heels, she stumbled and fell flat in front of him. Her co-star, a superbly muscled specimen with better equipment below than above, didn't even look back to see what had caused the commotion in his wake.

As she struggled to stand without flashing the picketers, Alan leaned down and offered her his hand. When his fellow protesters saw this, they collectively created a pocket of oxygen deprivation that would have caused a small child to pass out.

"Hate the sin, not the sinner," Alan said loudly. "This young woman is not the enemy -- she is a lost lamb seeking her Shepherd."

Evelyn, on her feet once again, heard the limo driver beep his horn in two short bursts. She was holding them up. Since neither the driver nor her misogynistic celluloid lover could be troubled to help her, she turned her back to the car and addressed Alan instead. "Thank you," she purred.

"Are you okay?" he asked. "That was a nasty spill."

"I'm better now." She brushed the dust from the front of her tight, hot-pink spandex dress.

Alan straightened and cleared his throat. "Are you lost?"

She flashed a half smile at him and perched her arm on her right hip. "That depends. Are you asking what a girl like me is doing in a place like this, or are you asking if I've met Hay-soos?"

His eyebrows drew together in puzzlement before his mind worked out what she had said. "Both," he answered simply.

"I'm here signing autographs, and Hay-soos played a voyeuristic janitor in my last flick."

He reached a finger up to loosen his collar, where it discovered he was wearing a v-neck tee shirt. He redirected his hand to his back pocket, pulling out his wallet. "Listen," he said as he opened the wallet, "my name is Reverend Alan Shaw. If you decide you would like to change your life, call me. No strings attached."

He wasn't the first man to offer to "rescue" her -- a rich old magazine magnate had offered her a place in his stable of women, a bartender invited her to live with him as his submissive, and the owner of an escort service promised she could make at least two grand a night. But Alan was the first one who offered to do it without anything in return. She took his card.

The limo driver revved his engine and blasted the horn for a long five seconds.

When the noise died away, she said, "Thanks," and teetered away.

In the car, the meatheaded "actor" asked, "Did you know that dude?"

She didn't answer him. She slid the card into her tiny matching handbag. "You carrying?"

"Do I look like a bedbug to you?"

She thought, but didn't say, that he did. However, she knew his drug of choice was steroids. "Not even some X?"

He rolled his eyes and said, "Yeah. I got some." He dug in his pocket and came up with a small tin that originally held Altoids. Popping the lid, he held it out to her.

"Thanks, man." She popped one and leaned her head back to wait for the euphoria to kick in.

"Give me a blow job for it?"

"Who are you kidding? I know you'd rather have the limo driver go down on you."

"A mouth's a mouth."

She sighed. "Fine. Give me a few minutes, though."

"Take your time. It's a long drive back to L.A."

# # #

She chose a flight scheduled to arrive an hour ahead of Desmond's. When she arrived at the large desert airport half an hour later than she expected, she sprinted from her arrival gate to his, hoping to meet her tall, muscular son as he deplaned. She arrived in time to see his plane taxi to the gate and breathed a sigh of relief. At least one of her plans had come out right. She sank into one of the black faux-leather seats near the ramp's exit door and waited.

She hadn't seen Des since Marty's funeral. Of her two children, he had always been the more forgiving of her faults, and, though she knew it was wrong, she loved him more than

Hope. Maybe it was because he was her youngest. Maybe it was because of his relaxed attitude toward life. Whatever it was, she always knew she could count on him to defend her against his sister's poison darts.

The plane began to empty. She knew instinctively that he would be one of the last off the vehicle. She watched as the surge of business types going home, vacationers anxious to feel the warmth of the desert's winter sun, and elderly snowbirds passed by. At last, Des, still solid as a block wall, appeared. Unexpectedly, he was holding a young, attractive woman's hand.

Unable to swallow, she stared as the couple passed by. A moment later, she saw her son's head swivel to look at her again. He smiled, bemused, and said something to his companion. She turned and looked as well, smiling and nodding.

Evelyn found her feet and walked quickly toward the strolling couple. The girl's smile faltered and she said something to Des, who quickly turned to face her.

"I'm so sorry, Miss. We didn't mean to stare. It's just that you look so much like my mother when she was younger."

"Desmond," she said softly.

His face creased with confusion. "How do you know my name?"

"It's me, Des. It's Mom."

His eyes widened in horror and he backed away, tripping over his own feet. His girlfriend was forced to steady him. "Look, lady, I don't know what kind of sick game--"

"Your favorite toys were Legos. Your imaginary friend was named Ricky." She searched her brain for other memories from his childhood. "You hate green beans because they squeak when you bite into them."

"Only when they aren't cooked long enough," he said. "Mom? Is that really you?"

She nodded.

"What the hell happened to you? Did you spend all of Marty's money on a complete surgical upgrade?"

"No. Of course not. I was sick. Cancer. I was going to die. Aunt Carmen got me into a clinical trial for a drug -- Promorterem. This...is what happened when I took it."

He shook his head. "I've never heard of this before. If you were part of a clinical trial, why isn't this all over the media?"

"It is. They call it the Cure for Death."

His girlfriend pulled on his arm. "I've heard of that," she said.

"Yeah. I have too. But all the experts say it can't be real. They say it's a hoax."

"They won't be saying that for much longer," Evelyn said.

"Can you get the drug for Dad?"

She cast her eyes downward. "No. I'm just a patient, Des. I don't have any power."

His eyes narrowed in suspicion. "How long have you been...like this?"

She swallowed her anxiety. "Almost three years now."

"And you didn't think your children might want to know?"

"I'm not supposed to seek out people who wouldn't normally be in my life."

Des straightened to his full height. "I want to be in your life! You're the only one stopping that! Hell, I didn't even know you were sick!"

"I didn't want you or Hope to know. After all that has passed between us...after I broke up our family...I didn't want you to come to my bedside out of some sort of misplaced guilt."

"We wouldn't have come out of guilt, Mom. At least, I wouldn't have." He gently pulled himself free of the young woman beside him and walked to Evelyn. Wrapping his strong arms around her, he pulled her into a hug.

Her head didn't even reach his shoulder. She marveled that such a child had come from her womb. "I've missed you, Des."

"Hope is going to blow a gasket when she sees you."

She squeezed him tightly before releasing him. "Yeah. I know."

He took her hand and led her to his girlfriend, who had been awkwardly trying to give them privacy by staring at nothing in particular. He wrapped his free arm around her and she smiled appreciatively. "Mom, this is Leah, my fiancee." He glanced down at her worriedly. "At least, I hope she still wants to marry me."

"Of course!" she said, elbowing him playfully. "You can't get rid of me just by introducing me to your younger and more beautiful mother!"

Des and Evelyn fidgeted uncomfortably at the girl's attempt at humor.

Leah turned neon pink.

Breaking the silence, Des said, "We need to get out of here. Do you need to go to baggage claim, Mom?"

"No. I've got everything right here," she said, patting the small carry-on bag slung over her shoulder. "You?"

"We're good to go. Let me call Glen so he can pull the car around." He pressed the button on his ear-phone and said, "Call Glen."

He walked a few paces away, leaving Evelyn with Leah. "When did you get engaged?" Evelyn asked, trying to be friendly to this awkward woman who would be her daughter-in-law.

"Just last week. We were at Machu Picchu when he suddenly--"

"You flew in from Peru?"

"Well...South America. We weren't really restricted to one country."

"How long have you known each other?"

"A while now."

"Where did you meet?"

"Caracas."

"Venezuela?"

She flashed an amused smile. "I don't know of any other Caracas, do you?"

Offhand, Evelyn couldn't think of another one. "How long have you been in South America?"

"A little over three months. I just graduated from college. As a graduation gift, my family gave me enough money to travel anywhere I wanted for six months. I chose South America."

"So you and Desmond have known each other three months?"

"Goodness, no!"

Evelyn breathed a sigh of relief. "So you met on a previous trip?"

She smiled gently, as if she were speaking to a child. "No. We met in Caracas, Venezuela. I already told you that. Do you think that drug they gave you might have affected your cognitive abilities?"

Evelyn sucked in her cheeks irritably before deciding to try another tack. "When were you in Caracas?"

"Oh! Last month. Why?"

Evelyn glanced toward her son, wondering if the proposal was simply a ploy to get in this girl's pants. Then again...she had noticed that her fellow students weren't exactly prudish. Most of the girls had no problem whatsoever with premarital sex, and Leah looked just like them. Besides, she couldn't see her sweet baby boy as a player. If anything, he was being played. "Where are you from?"

"Virginia. Why?"

"No reason. You have a lovely accent."

The girl laughed. "Compared to some Southern girls, I barely have a drawl."

Having run out of conversation, Evelyn smiled and looked again toward her son, who was now returning to them.

29

"He'll be there in five minutes. Come on, ladies, we have a hike to make."

As she struggled to keep up with Des' long stride, she asked, "Did you prepare Glen?"

"I mentioned you looked younger than ever, but I think he thought I was kidding."

The threesome made it to the designated exit doors in almost five minutes. Glen was already waiting at the curb. Desmond easily lifted Evelyn and Leah's bags from their shoulders and the two women slid into the backseat of the car as Des deposited the bags in the trunk.

"Where's Evelyn?" Glen asked as Desmond stepped into the front of the vehicle.

"Right behind you," he said.

Glen glanced up at his rear-view mirror. Evelyn saw the color drain from his face. "What in God's name did you do to yourself?"

"I had a little work done," she lied.

"A little? My God, they must have left half of your skin on the surgical floor. Does Hope know?"

"Not yet."

He closed his eyes and rubbed his temples. "I feel a migraine coming on."

"Want me to drive, man?" Des asked.

Glen straightened and pulled away from the curb both hands now firmly on the wheel. "Nope. But when you go in the house, be sure to tell Hope I had some errands to run."

#

Hope and Glen had moved since the last time Evelyn had been to visit them. Their new home was bright and airy, taking advantage of the latest developments in smart-glass technology. The home seemed to be made almost entirely of glass. Evelyn couldn't help but wonder how they kept cool in the summer months. She was tempted to pick up a stone and throw it at the house, just to see if the glass was truly as strong and damage resistant as she had been led to believe by the home shows on television.

Glen drove away before Hope even reached the front door to greet Des, Leah, and Evelyn. Evie could see her daughter as she approached the door. She was an attractive, if dour, woman. Evie remembered how many times she had told her daughter to smile more often; Hope never really mastered the art of a sweet countenance. As soon as she saw her brother through the glass though, her face lit up. Evelyn saw her lips move and the door slid open.

"Des!" she said as she threw her arms around his neck. "I'm so glad you came." She pulled back and looked at him. "Have you been taking care of yourself? You look older."

"I am older, sis. You look terrific."

She twirled and said, "Glen got me a personal trainer for Christmas." As if for the first time, she looked at Leah and Evelyn. "Where's Mom? Oh, let me guess: something came up." She pursed her lips and her eyelids drooped down over her green eyes.

Desmond turned and looked at his mother with expectation.

Evelyn looked behind her, wishing she could find an escape route. There was none to be found -- Glen was long gone and the wide expanse of lawn hindered her from hiding effectively. Taking a deep breath, she said, "I'm right here, Hope."

Her daughter's expression flickered from confusion to disbelief to amazement before settling on anger. "What the hell did you do to yourself?"

Hope's daughter appeared behind her, no doubt curious about her mother's obvious distress. When she saw Desmond, she snaked under her mom's arms -- which were perched indignantly on her hips -- and threw herself at Desmond. "Uncle Des!"

"Abby!" he answered, hugging her tightly.

"Come and hug Grandma, Abigail," Evelyn said, smiling brightly.

The girl frowned and backed up a step. "Who are you?"

"I'm your grandmother."

She backed up another step and looked at her mother, who wore a matching expression.

"It's okay," Des said. "It's really her, Hope. I swear to God."

With one more glance at her mother, Abby stepped forward and hugged Evelyn gingerly.

Hope stood to one side and said, "You might as well come in."

Though she hadn't been able to see through the glass from the outside, inside the house, Evelyn was amazed to see that the walls allowed a clear view of the beautifully landscaped yard. Opaque glass walls separated the rooms into traditional spaces. Family photographs and classical art images seemed to float on the large screens. Hope led them into the living room, where Evelyn settled into a comfortable orange chair. Desmond and Leah sat side by side on the matching low sofa.

"Abby, would you bring our guests something to drink?"

"I'll just have water," Desmond said. Leah nodded in agreement. "Make that two, Abby."

"Sure, Uncle Des. Um...Grandma?"

"Do you have some coffee?"

"I can make you a cup," the girl offered.

Evelyn couldn't remember how old the girl was. Twelve? Thirteen? Old enough, she decided. "Yes, please. With a little Irish cream in it if you don't mind."

"The Bailey's is in Dad's office, Abby," Hope said.

The girl left the room.

"Explain this, please." Hope leaned against one of the glass walls. The electronics contained within it sent a ripple out as if it were a pond responding to a pebble. The ripple echoed silently across the walls.

"I was sick," Evelyn began. She told her children and Leah everything.

By the time she finished, Hope had slid to the floor, her knees in front of her. Abby, a loyal child, sat next to her. Hope grasped her hand and asked, "How do we get the Cure for Dad?"

Evelyn shook her head. "We can't."

"That can't be true! If there's a cure out there, we can afford it. Glen and I -- we have plenty of money. More than enough to buy this drug."

"It's not available yet."

"Anything can be gotten for a price," she scoffed. "I'll have a dose before nightfall!" She pushed herself up resolutely and exited the room.

Abby remained on the floor chewing on her lip nervously.

"Abby," Evelyn asked, "would you take me to see your grandpa now?"

She looked up, meeting Evelyn's eyes for the first time. "So, you won't die for a long time now?"

"No. It's like I'm young again. I have another fifty or sixty years at least."

Abby smiled. "That's amazing."

"I agree."

Abby stood up and took Evelyn by the hand. "Come on, Grandma. Grandpa's been waiting for you."

#

The walls in Alan's room were darkened to keep the harsh light from bothering him, though they weren't opaque. Instead, it was as if his bedroom were surrounded by a garden perpetually lit by only the moon.

"Grandpa?" Abby called.

"He's not here," Alan answered. His voice was scuffed with age, but the cadence and accent of his words were recognizable to Evelyn.

"Go on back to the others," Evelyn said quietly, patting the girl's shoulder.

Abby nodded and retreated.

As soon as she disappeared down the hall, Evelyn closed the door to Alan's room and said, "I'm sorry I'm so late, Alan."

He turned over in his bed and looked up at her. "Why do you stay out all night, Evelyn? Don't you know how much I miss you?"

"I'm sorry. You're a good man. I should have treated you better."

He patted the bed next to him. "Come sit with me."

She walked over and sat down. She allowed herself to study his face. He had never been particularly handsome -- his eyes were too close together and his nose was hawkish -- but age sat well on him. Hardships hadn't hardened his soul. Maybe the Alzheimer's helped in that respect. After all, one can't resent what one can't remember. She took his hand between her own. "How are you feeling?"

"Well enough," he answered. He pulled his hand away and tried to push himself up in bed, but he couldn't seem to get enough traction against the soft blankets.

"Lean forward," she said, grabbing an extra pillow from the chair nearby. She put the pillow behind him and sat down again.

"That's better," Alan said. He closed his eyes for a second; Evelyn wondered if he was going to fall asleep. She was about to stand and leave the room when his eyes popped open again. "How is it that you are still so beautiful after all these years?"

"You look at me through your love, Alan. No one else has ever done that for me."

His eyes narrowed. "Hand me a mirror."

She looked around the room, but there were none to be seen. Finally, she pulled her phone from her purse and turned on the camera function. She handed it to him.

As he studied the screen, the corners of his mouth fell. "I'm old," he whispered. "I'm so very old. And you've been gone for so many years, sweet Evelyn. I should have paid more attention -- I should have known you were unhappy."

"I'm here now."

"No...you're just an illusion. Just another sign of this twisted disease." He let the hand holding her phone fall to his lap. He reached for the buzzer sitting on the small table to his right.

Evelyn took her phone from his other hand and slipped her fingers into his palm, pressing them there tightly. "Alan," she said sharply, "look at me. I'm not an illusion. I'm here."

He stopped and looked into her eyes. "Then why do you look like that? You look younger than the first time I met you!"

"Let's not dwell on that. We have so much to say...let's not worry about appearances."

He brought his right hand back to the bed. "Okay. Tell me why you left."

#

The first time she called Alan after meeting him in his picket line, she was high on something that made her feel like the world was made of cotton candy clouds. They talked for hours.

When he called her the next day, she barely remembered their previous conversation, but she understood that this man wasn't only interested in fucking a porn star; he saw something in her that she had forgotten existed. She kept talking to him.

A few months later, she was picked up for possession. She would have called her "manager," the same asshole who had recruited her into the business five years earlier, if it hadn't been for the cop who interrogated her.

"Evie," he said at the end of the interview, "don't you have anyone else you can call? If you keep living like this, you're going to be dead before you're twenty-five."

She took his words as prophetic and dialed Alan instead.

And he was her savior: he bailed her out, put her in rehab, and visited her as often as the program would allow. When she was clean, he took her back to Phoenix and found her a room in one of his congregation members' homes. The Winslows were a kind, older couple with a housecleaning business; she went to work for them making ten percent of what she once made as a porn star. At the end of each week she would take the meager amount of cash and mourn briefly for the life she had once known. But she still believed that Alan saved her, so she dutifully put ten percent in the plate every Sunday and hung on Reverend Alan's words. She accepted Christ just to feel Alan's hands on her as he dipped her into the cool water of the baptismal pool. She fantasized about giving him a blow job as he stood at the pulpit, but she kept that thought to herself.

After six months, Alan began courting her, though she hadn't recognized that he was doing so. He came to dinner at the Winslow home every Sunday for two months before asking her to be his date at a church function.

There were, of course, some whispers and gossip, but Alan was quick to gently nudge the congregation from their hypocrisy into acceptance. He preached more than once about forgiveness and being made new in Christ. She didn't feel new...but she did feel forgiven. She imagined their life together: a wholesome family with green grass in the yard and a home so full of happiness that the excess would spill out the door every time they opened it. She imagined that her life would be just like that of the princesses in fairytales: she would become queen of the congregation and live happily ever after.

For a while, her fairytale ending seemed true. Alan married her and they had two perfect children. The congregation accepted her as Reverend Alan's wife, and she sat in the front row every Sunday, one child on each side, for years. She relished her role as the women's de facto leader. She loved the praise heaped on her for living such a morally upright life and showing the true redemptive power of Christ's love.

But forty snuck up on Evelyn like a ninja. One day she was young and vibrant, happily raising Hope and Desmond and glorying in her remarkable transformation; the next, she was sobbing into the sofa pillows and wondering where she took the wrong turn. She began going out at night. She told Alan that she was spending time with other women in the congregation -- first one, then another. But he saw those women every Wednesday and Sunday, and it wasn't long before he asked one of them how their night out with Evelyn had been.

He waited up one night until she snuck quietly through the door like a teenager breaking curfew. "Evelyn," he said softly from just a few feet away.

She jumped a foot off the ground. "What are you doing up?"

"I know you weren't out with Barb. I called her a few hours ago."

"What are you doing? Checking up on me?" She felt guilt and anger swirling within her. "I'm your wife, Alan -- not your child!"

"Don't yell," he answered. "Don't wake the children."

"They're teenagers. I think they should know by now that adults fight." She wanted to scream the words, but she forced herself to use a reasonable tone.

"Where were you?"

"Out."

"Who were you with?"

"No one."

His eyes scanned her body; Evelyn wanted to cover the too-short dress and hide the ridiculously high platform heels -- shoes that changed her from a five-foot-five housewife into a five-foot-eleven playgirl -- behind her. "What's wrong?" he asked plaintively. "What has changed? I thought you -- we -- were happy! I love you so much, Evie. Why don't you want to be here with me?"

She bent her knees until she could set the shoes quietly on the floor. Her hands empty, she went to him and sat in his lap, wrapping her arms around him. "I'm sorry, Alan. I really am. I don't know what's wrong with me."

"Just...stay home, darling. I miss you, the children miss you. We want you here."

Instead of answering him, she kissed him, allowing her mouth to open against the pressure of his.

A moment later, he recoiled in disgust. "Were you smoking?"

The blood drained from her face as she recalled her evening and the handsome man with the bad habit who had done more than just kiss her.

Alan dumped her from his lap, leaving her crumpled on the floor. "I'm going to bed. You find someplace else to sleep."

# # #

Evelyn held her ex-husband's hand as he drifted to sleep. The regret that coursed through her veins wasn't for leaving him, but for ever entangling him in her life in the first place. If not for her, he might have a wife next to him as he lay dying. At least he had their children -- even Desmond, who had always been a momma's boy. She had lost them all -- gambled them away on a bet that she was missing something by being a wife and mother.

When she felt his grip loosen and heard his soft snores, she pulled her hand away and left him. Back in the living room, her son sat quietly on the sofa with Leah's hand in his own.

Abby was sitting in one of the orange chairs with a reading device. When she saw Evelyn, she put it down and asked, "Does he need something?"

"No. He's asleep."

The girl nodded solemnly.

"You're close to him, huh?"

"He doesn't remember me...not really. Usually, he calls me Hope. Mom thinks it's because I look a lot like her when she was my age."

Evelyn didn't agree. Hope had inherited her father's too-close eyes. Abby's eyes were more like Glen's -- big, round, and widely spaced. "It's good of you to take care of him like you do."

She shrugged. "I don't do much. Mom does almost everything for him."

Hope, the rims of her eyes red as a stop sign, came around the corner. "Glen is going to get it," she said, though her voice wavered.

Evelyn frowned, but didn't correct her.

"What, Mom?" she said angrily. "Spit it out."

"It's not approved by the FDA yet, sweetheart. I don't think--"

"Don't you call me by your pet names! I'm not your sweetheart! I'm only your daughter because we share genetic material! The only relief I've had in this whole fucking nightmare has been knowing that you would be dead before I would! And now...what the hell kind of justice is this? You're going to fucking outlive me!" Hope sank to the floor. Abby flashed an angry glance at Evelyn before going to her mother and wrapping her arms around her.

Hope sucked in a breath, opened her eyes, and saw her daughter beside her. She pulled the girl to her and sobbed on her shoulder.

"I should go," Evelyn said.

"Mom," Des asked, "where are you going? Your flight doesn't leave for two days."

"I'll get a hotel room. Your sister clearly doesn't want me here."

"This isn't about what Hope wants."

Hope sucked in a ragged breath.

"I'm sorry, sis, but it's not. This is about making a dying man happy, and you're just about the only person on the planet who can do that."

Evelyn swallowed. "He doesn't want to see me. He just wants to know that what happened wasn't his fault."

"How could he doubt that?" Hope had released her daughter and was now staring up at them. "You cheated on him, not the other way around!"

"He would have forgiven her," Des said. "You know Dad loved Mom so much he would have forgiven her for anything."

"He told me to find somewhere else to sleep," Evelyn said quietly.

"He didn't mean outside the house, Mom."

"Yes, he did."

"The morning after you left, he tried like hell to find you. He called everyone he could think of looking for you."

Evelyn remembered that morning. She sat in a rundown coffee shop along Grand Avenue for hours, watching the blue-collar workers eat their eggs and flirt with the waitresses, most of whom were taking their style cues from Donna Reed and Lydia the Tattooed Lady. When she finally made up her mind to leave Phoenix, she walked to the nearby bus terminal and caught the first one headed north. "I left the city before the end of the day."

"You abandoned us!" Hope wailed. "How could you just leave?"

"You two were almost grown! You didn't need me anymore. I was tired of trying to be someone I wasn't. Alan may not remember it that way now, but he was glad to see me go." She pulled out her phone and said into it, "Call taxi service."

Desmond grabbed the phone away from her and cancelled the call. "No. You aren't running away from this, Mom. Pretty soon, you're going to be the only parent we have left."

"Jesus Christ, Desmond. Let her go," Hope said. "She looks young enough to be our sister. She's not a mother anymore."

Desmond, slack-jawed, relaxed the hand holding Evelyn's phone. She took it back and again commanded the phone to call for a taxi service.

"Are you really leaving?" Abby asked. Her big eyes showed her hurt clearly.

"Yes. But I'll keep in touch this time."

"What about Grandpa? Don't you think you should say goodbye?"

"Oh, honey...we said goodbye a long time ago."

# # #

"What are you doing here?" Carmen asked, her arms crossed over her chest. She didn't move to unblock her doorway and let Evelyn inside.

"My marriage is over."

"You left Alan?"

Evelyn turned and looked back at the street on which Carmen's house was located. "This is a nice place. I always thought you preferred being closer to your work though."

"I don't work at the hospital anymore. I opened my own practice a few years back...which you would know if you ever called me."

"I've been a little busy."

"And I haven't? I'm the doctor, you know. You were just a housewife."

Her eyes widened as she whirled on her sister. "Just a housewife?! I wish! If I had been 'just a housewife' I might still be with Alan! Instead, I've been the role model for an entire congregation -- a physical representation of redemption for a hundred women. My house had to be clean all the time. My children had to be perfect. My devotion to Alan had to seem unbreakable. My...life...had to be..." She sank down to the tile-covered step on which she had been standing. "Perfect," she muttered as her eyes welled with tears. She pressed her palms against them and wished for her happily ever after.

She felt the heat of Carmen's body next to her and looked at her sister. Carmen had an air of authority about her -- she always had. Her salt-and-pepper hair only intensified that characteristic. "I'm sorry," she said. "I just missed you. I haven't seen you since Dad's funeral. The only reason I knew you were still alive was because you kept sending Christmas cards."

"I missed you too. But I didn't want you to know how screwed up I was."

"Better that I know it than for you to keep it a secret. Look what happened to Karen."

She nodded. Their sister Karen had committed suicide not long after Evelyn got clean. She hadn't wanted their family to know that she had dug herself into a financial hole she couldn't climb out of.

"What about your faith? Aren't there rules about marriages? Aren't you supposed to work through your problems and avoid divorce?"

"I don't think I ever really believed all that."

"So Jesus Christ isn't your savior?"

42

"No. And neither was Alan."

Carmen wrapped her arm around Evelyn's shoulders. "Welcome home, baby girl."

The cab dropped her off at her dormitory at eleven-thirty Sunday evening. She called Arleta, who came down and opened the door for her. "Everything okay?" asked her sleepy roommate.

"Yeah. Sorry. I couldn't remember my code."

"No problem," Arleta said over a yawn. "I just turned out the lights a few minutes ago."

"Sure you did," Evelyn laughed. Together, they walked toward the stairs leading to their room.

"How was your family?"

"They're okay."

"Really? I got the impression something was wrong. I mean, it's not like you were planning to go home in the middle of the semester."

"I guess not. But it wasn't anything terrible. Just, you know, time marching on."

Arleta looked at her quizzically, but didn't ask any more questions. "You got a call from the radio station. I think you might have gotten the job."

"Really?" Evelyn's exhaustion ebbed away. "Why didn't you call me?"

"They only called this morning. I knew you'd be back tonight."

"What makes you think I got it?"

"You think they call people to tell them they didn't get the job?"

"Wow."

"Yeah...that's awesome, Evie. You're on your way!"

As soon as they reached their room, Arleta collapsed back into her bed. "Good night."

"Good night. And thanks."

"Yeah, anytime," she mumbled against her pillow.

Evelyn lay down on her bed, fully clothed, and stared up at the ceiling. In the dorm room, she couldn't help but think that the whole weekend was no more than a bad dream. After all, she wasn't old enough to have a teenaged granddaughter or a septuagenarian ex-husband. She was Evelyn Bryant, future television news anchor. She let the past drift away on the tide of her dreams for her future.

Chapter 4 Julian

Birdsong woke her the next morning. Arleta was already gone -- she had mostly morning classes. Her thoughtful roommate had put a blanket over Evelyn before she left; Evelyn popped out of bed, folded the cover, and draped it across Arleta's bed.

At first, she couldn't put her finger on what was different; she only knew that she felt better. She showered and changed into a clean pair of jeans and a t-shirt, pulled her thick, sable hair into a ponytail, and walked to the commons to get breakfast.

As she sat down in a comfortable chair with her bagel and coffee, a young man looked up from his reading device and smiled. "Evelyn, right?"

"Yes," she answered, grinning in return. He was news-anchor handsome -- all white teeth and perfect blond hair. "Aren't you Professor Andres' teaching assistant?"

He nodded. "So you have noticed me!"

She laughed lightly. "It's hard not to. You sit at the front of the room behind a desk."

"Practicing for my future as a reporter. That's what Andres calls it, anyway." He set the reading device in his lap and stuck out a hand. "Julian Harris."

She set her coffee and bagel on the arm of the chair and met his hand. "Pleasure. Now, how is it you recognize me out of all of Andres' hundreds of students?"

"That's easy -- you're the one she pointed out to me on the first day."

Evelyn straightened self-consciously. "Why would she do that?"

"She said you were the one to watch -- the one with a future in journalism."

She blushed as the compliment hit home. Evelyn had watched Crista Andres on network television every morning when she was raising Hope and Desmond. She thought of the woman as an old friend -- someone she shared mornings with. Alan had commented more than once on how similar the two women appeared, and Evelyn was always flattered that he thought she was so beautiful. When Crista disappeared from the network a few years ago, Evelyn -- and many others -- felt the loss of her calm, pleasant presence. A lot of people assumed that she was fired because of her age -- she was at least sixty now. In fact, the network would have kept her forever if she hadn't been in a disfiguring accident. Her once-attractive face was now deeply scarred. Since she couldn't do what she loved anymore, she taught others how to do it. "Wow!" she finally managed to say.

"Yeah, it's rare that she points someone out like that. I wouldn't doubt her words, though. Did you know that Kayla Sykes was one of her students? Andres once brought Kayla to the front of the class and announced that they were looking at the next Barbara Walters!"

Invoking Barbara Walters' name in a media class is like naming a theology student as the next messiah. Evelyn's jaw dropped and her eyes bugged out. "Were you there for that?" she whispered.

He laughed. "Of course not. That was ten years ago. But the moment is legendary...and, of course, Kayla's definitely taken up the Walters mantle."

Evelyn fell back into her chair, raising her elbows as she did so. The forgotten coffee hit the floor with a loud clatter and liquid-brown spreading splatter.

"Hey!" screeched the girl in the seat to the right as the coffee droplets stained her hippie-style skirt and retro backpack.

"Shit! Sorry," Evelyn said.

Shooting her a dirty look, one of the barristas came out from behind the counter with a mop.

She sighed and looked for Julian, whom she fully expected to find exiting the shop. Instead, he was smirking at her from the same chair he had been in before.

He held out his hand again. "Here," he said, "let me take you out for a real breakfast instead."

She nodded as she let him help her up. "That sounds delightful." Leaving her bagel still balanced on the armchair, they left the mess behind them.

As her past receded from her mind, Evelyn was pleased to have Julian fill her present. At first, she thought of him as just a friend -- he was much too young to be anything else. But he was smart, well-read, and handsome. He was more than polite to mousy Arleta -- he was kind. And, little by little, he wore her down with his bright smile and cheery demeanor. It didn't hurt that so many of their media-major classmates commented on how television-ready their relationship was.

Evelyn woke up one morning in late spring and realized she was in love with Julian, a man younger than her own son. At that same moment, fear struck her for the first time as it occurred to her that he didn't really know her. And, she resolved, he never could.

"Welcome to Vegas, baby!" Julian announced as Evelyn ran into his arms.

47

"God, but I've missed you!" she said, burying her head against his neck and inhaling deeply. It had been most of a year since she had been in her lover's arms. After nearly a year of applications and rejections, he had taken a reporting position in the large market right before the start of her junior year of college. Hologram sexual play turned out to be largely dissatisfying and troublesome, especially with a roommate. After a few attempts, they just kept their clothes on. Now, with just one year to finish on her college degree, she was spending the summer with Julian in Vegas.

Julian looked well, if a little slicker than he had the year before. She supposed Vegas did that to a person. She had only been to the city once before, when she was much older and engaged to Marty. She wasn't much of a gambler, but Marty had liked to play craps. She stood by and blew on his dice for him. He took her to a few of the big shows and bought her a ruby ring. The hotel they had stayed in was opulently gaudy. They had agreed, after that one trip, that Vegas wasn't really their kind of town.

Julian took her hand and led her out into the clear Vegas sun. He had a car waiting for them. The driver took her bag and they slipped into the car and each other's arms. With a flick of his finger, Julian rolled up the darkened window between them and the driver. Then he slipped that hand between her legs. "I have missed you so much," he said as his hand neared the warmth between her thighs.

She opened her legs like a flower blooming under the hot desert sun. "Oh, Julian," she moaned, "I can't believe how long it's been."

He pulled his hand back and smiled regretfully. "Don't get too revved up, sweetheart. I'm afraid we have a party to go to."

Taken aback, she pulled her legs together and straightened in the seat. "But I just got off a plane!" she objected. "I look awful!"

"Evelyn, you have never looked awful in your life. You just need a little color on your face. Even the dress you're wearing is perfect."

She looked down at her loose floral print travel dress and frowned. "I wore this because it was comfortable. I can't meet people in it!"

He rolled the window between them and the driver down again. "Change of plans. Run us by the house, okay?"

"Yes, Mr. Harris," the driver answered with a nod.

"You have a house?"

"You're going to love it," he said. "I picked it out with you in mind. It's a turn-of-the-century Modern with tons of space."

When they pulled up in front of it, Evie looked out and thought *McMansion*. That's what her parents would have called a place like this: a huge house on less than an acre of land. Still, it was pretty and not a dorm room. She leaned over and kissed Julian on the cheek. "It's lovely."

He beamed with pride. "Wait until you see the inside!"

She stepped out of the limo and walked up the cement pathway to the front door while Julian and the driver handled her bag. A moment later, Julian was at the door with the key in his hand and her bag over his shoulder. He unlocked the house and pushed open one side of the double doors. The foyer was two stories high and painted a sunny yellow. The flooring that stretched before her was terra cotta Mexican tile. To one side was some kind of Day-of-the-Dead-style painting. She could see he had really taken a liking to all things Hispanic. Having grown up in Phoenix, she was less entranced by those things.

"What do you think?" he asked nervously.

"It's very nice," she answered.

"We're going to be so happy here! Las Vegas is like paradise -- no one judges anyone! Everyone is happy!"

"Except the poor suckers who lost their last dime in the casinos," she said wryly.

"Those aren't locals," he scoffed. "The locals are always happy."

She resisted the urge to roll her eyes at her naive boyfriend. "I need to freshen up. Where--?"

He led her to the stairs. "Up there, on the right. Use the master bedroom suite."

She went up the stairs and found more terra cotta flooring. The bedroom itself was painted a pale-orangey color. A yellow shag rug covered almost half the floor and was surrounded on three sides by rustic-looking leather furniture, all of which seemed to be focused on the natural stone fireplace. The other half of the room was filled with a king-sized bed set on an overwhelming lodge-pole frame. Evelyn wondered briefly why anyone would need so much seating in a room that was essentially meant for only two people.

In the attached bathroom -- which was itself larger than the room she shared with Arleta -- she found a bathtub big enough for three and a shower the size of a walk-in closet. She shook her head, wondering exactly how Julian had grown up. He had never introduced her to any of his family. As far as she knew, none of them had even attended his graduation. He told her he was from Kentucky originally, but by the time she met him, his accent was something he only pulled out as a party trick to amuse his friends.

She settled in front of the mirrored wall and pulled her makeup out of her bag. She applied fresh lipstick and eyeliner. She pulled her hair out of its ponytail and brushed it before deciding that she would need to put it up again. She fashioned it into a french roll and clipped it. Taking a moment to admire herself in the mirror, she was pleased with what she saw: her heart-shaped face with a dimpled instead of pointed chin, her bow-shaped lips, and her thick sable-brown hair. She had never looked this good back when she was a porn star. Thankfully, her legacy of smut was long-forgotten after more than forty years out of the business. No one had recognized her as Evie Amour since Hope and Desmond were small.

She carefully pulled the loose-fitting dress over her head and opened up her bag to extract a more suitable outfit for a Las Vegas party. She wiggled into the tight-fitting red-sequined number she had been carrying around with her for most of her life -- a relic of racier days. She had stuffed it in her bag at the last minute, figuring that if she were going to wear red sequins anywhere, Las Vegas was the most likely spot. She giggled, realizing that the dress and the house were likely of the same vintage. She pulled a pair of all-purpose clear dress heels with rhinestone detailing out and slipped them on. Finally, she added the jewelry Marty had bought her years before in this same city. She fingered the ruby ring lovingly, remembering how good her second husband had been to her. She still missed him sometimes, though much of her past seemed like no more than a series of dream images.

Her heels clacked on the tile as she headed down the stairs. Julian appeared from deeper in the house and whistled his appreciation.

"You look phenomenal."

"It's not too much?"

"For Vegas? Babe, you may be underdressed. That's vintage, isn't it?"

"It's a few years old, but I wouldn't say--"

"That's okay. The Twenties are cool again...at least this season."

"So where are we going?"

"It's a network party. All the bigwigs are in town for a convention, and I was invited to represent the Las Vegas talent." He preened like a peacock.

"Why you? What about the regular anchor?"

"I'm that guy -- as of next week."

She rushed down the stairs and threw her arms around him. "Oh, baby...I'm so proud of you!"

"I was going to let it be a surprise," he said against her neck.

"I'm not surprised. You belong on an anchor desk."

"Let's go," he said, giving her a quick squeeze. "We're going to be late."

#

The party was full of men in suits and women in glitzy, if conservative, dresses. Julian's boss, a youngish hawk-like woman dressed in a cream-colored frock with brown detailing, looked Evelyn over as if she were a side of beef she was considering butchering for steak.

"So, this is the famous Evelyn." She sipped what could have just been a diet soda, but Evelyn guessed had a fair portion of rum in it.

"How do you do?" she asked amiably.

"Quite well, thank you. We just love Julian here. He's so...wholesome, wouldn't you agree?"

"And talented as well."

"Of course. But then, how much talent does it take to look cute and read?"

Julian laughed, but Evelyn wanted to kick the snide bitch. "It was nice to meet you," she said. "Julian, perhaps you could--"

"Wait," said the rude woman, putting a hand on her shoulder to stop her from walking away. "Julian tells me that you are in school to become a news presenter too."

She counted to three before she turned around again. "Yes."

"The owner of the station has been trying to come up with a cutesy ploy for a while now. I can't think of anything cuter than a married news team. Maybe you and loverboy should get hitched."

"Are you suggesting," Julian interjected, "that if we were married, Evelyn could be my new co-anchor?"

"I'm saying that she'd have first shot at the job...should that seat become available."

"Is that seat going to be available soon?"

The white witch smiled. "You know how...changeable executive minds can be. Excuse me -- I need a word with the Chicago station manager and I see him right there." She brushed passed Evelyn. "Yoo hoo! Charles! Over here!"

Evelyn turned to Julian. "Is she serious?"

"As a heart attack. She told me six months ago that I should bide my time -- the anchor job would be coming my way."

"Why didn't you mention that to me?"

"I didn't have the job yet, did I?" He pulled me to the far corner of the room. "Megan found out I was applying for better positions in other markets. She knew what I wanted was the anchor job. And she knows I want you here."

"What do you give her in exchange?"

The hesitation was so brief, Evelyn wasn't positive it was there. "Nothing. She just wants the Vegas market sewn up, and nothing sells here like beauty and sex."

"So? Don't you have chemistry with the current co-anchor?"

He frowned. "Not really. She's still pissed that Joe was shown the door, and I think she's a little paranoid that she's about to follow him out it."

"I don't think that's paranoia she's experiencing," Evelyn said wryly. "I think I'd call that a premonition."

He shrugged. "Maybe, maybe not."

"Did you not just hear Megan say--"

"Yeah, but nothing is written in stone. Jordan would have to do something serious to find herself out of a job. She's one of the most popular news personalities in Vegas." He took her hand and smiled. "Don't worry. Even if there's not a spot next to me at the desk, there will be a place at the station for you. Besides, you've got another year of college before you can even consider looking for a job."

"Andres didn't finish college. Look where she is now."

"Yeah, but times were different. When she was the lead anchor at NBC, no one expected anchors to understand the news -- just look pretty and read."

"Isn't that what Megan said your job was?"

"Yes, but she was being facetious."

An older, elegant woman was approaching them. Evelyn could see her over Julian's shoulder. "Someone is coming."

Julian pasted on his smile and turned around. "Jordan! What a surprise! I thought you didn't do these corporate parties anymore."

"Desperate times call for desperate measures," purred the brown-skinned Jordan. Her eyes were hypnotic -- slanted slightly upward and emerald green. "Is this your lady love?"

"Yes. Jordan, Evelyn. Evelyn, Jordan. Jordan is my co-anchor."

"It's a pleasure to meet you," Evelyn said, holding out a hand.

"You're as lovely as Julian said you were. You know, you look like a young Crista Andres." The woman smiled, showing her beautifully white teeth.

"Thank you. That's quite a compliment. Professor Andres is a great inspiration to me."

"Oh! You're one of her students! How lucky for you. I always wanted the opportunity to work with her. But," she sighed, allowing her eyes to drift over the crowd, "I ended up stuck in Vegas. Not exactly the network news desk, is it?" A musical laugh floated out of her.

Evelyn understood why this woman was beloved. She was charming, beautiful, and self-effacing. She would never do anything that would jeopardize her standing with her fan base. The only way she was leaving the anchor desk was in a funeral procession. The best Evelyn could hope for here was a shot at the local morning show -- and that wasn't where she wanted to spend her career.

"I'll leave you two lovebirds alone," she said sweetly. "Enjoy your summer, Evelyn. Make sure Julian takes you just everywhere in Vegas. Don't let him squirrel you away in that house of his." She winked at Julian and walked away.

"Megan is off her rocker if she thinks Jordan is leaving the news desk."

Julian smiled. "I tend to agree, but I wouldn't bet against Megan."

The next evening, Evelyn settled on the leather couch in the master suite and turned on the television above the fireplace -- which was cleverly disguised as a painting, of course -- to watch Julian read the news. The thing that was apparent almost immediately was that Jordan, not Julian, was the true lead anchor. She commanded the screen in a way that Julian just couldn't yet.

"Good evening. Thousands gathered in New York today..."

Evelyn admired the smooth silk of her voice and her calm demeanor. This woman should have made the network broadcast; there was no reason for her to be stuck in Las Vegas, unless this is what she chose.

As the news report continued, Evelyn's mind wandered. She suspected Julian, who had been so mature and in control back at college, had lost his way in this neon jungle. He was so busy molding himself into who he thought the station wanted that he had lost something of his own character. And she had to wonder how Megan and Jordan both knew so much about where Julian lived. She shuddered to think of Megan on her side of the bed.

She turned off the television and stripped down. Digging in her bag, she found her bikini and slipped it on. Padding down the chilly tiled steps and through the foyer that led into the great room, she tried not to notice its hollowness.

At least the house had a tall privacy wall -- no one at street level would be watching her late-night swim. Of course, with these McMansions, the neighbors could always see you, but she supposed if one of them was so bored that they were staring out their windows hoping to see a pretty woman, let them. She stepped onto the diving board and plunged into the cool water below.

A previous owner -- the one who had built the pool -- had invested in a retro mosaic on the bottom of it: a school of fish being chased by a whale. She didn't think that whales actually chased fish, but the tile work was attractive. She ran her fingers over the tiles in the whale's tail before pushing herself back to the surface.

As soon as the water drained from her ears, she could hear the crickets singing. She felt at peace -- completely calm for the first time since she was cured of cancer. She let herself float on the surface of the water. Maybe she could make a life here.

###

"Hello?"

"Evelyn, this is Jordan. Julian's co-anchor?"

"Of course! How are you?"

"I'm fine. The real question of the day is how are you? You must be bored out of your mind just hanging around that musty old house of his."

"I'm okay. I knew I'd be alone a lot of the time."

"Well, I have the day off. My daughter and I are planning a shopping trip on the Strip. We'd love for you to join us."

Evelyn hesitated. "I wouldn't want to interrupt your mother-daughter time."

"Not at all! You and Ronnie are about the same age. I think you'll get along famously."

Evelyn grimaced. She didn't need any more friends "her own age," but Jordan was right about her going a little stir-crazy. "Sounds like fun."

"Great. We'll pick you up in an hour."

"Who was that?" Julian asked as he padded into the kitchen.

She glanced at the clock: ten in the morning. "You're up early."

"The phone woke me up."

"I'm sorry...I thought I had the volume low enough."

"It's all right." He opened the fridge and pulled out a green smoothie -- his regular breakfast choice. "So? Who was on the phone?"

"Jordan. She invited me to go shopping with her."

He laughed. "Cozying up to the competition? Seems a little dangerous." He twisted the lid off the bottle and took a swig.

She walked behind him and laced her hands around his mid-section, feeling the developing abs under her fingers. She missed his softer, pre-career body. This one made her feel like she should be working out more. "She's just being friendly. She knows I'm on my own."

He turned in her arms. "You're not alone. You have me."

For a moment, she saw a glimpse of the boy she fell in love with. She smiled. "I like you like this."

"What does that mean?"

"You know...protective, warm...more like you used to be."

He leaned away from her, breaking out of her arms. "I don't think I'm any different now."

"You are," she said, frowning. "It's like you're becoming plastic."

His face fell and she could see where his wrinkles would eventually form. "I'm not. I'm exactly the same guy. I just had to grow up, that's all."

"Growing up doesn't mean becoming fake."

He walked away from her, toward the French doors that led to the pool. "You're being ridiculous," he said over his shoulder. "What would you know about growing up, anyway?" He slammed the door behind him.

"A lot more than you," she said to the empty room. Disheartened, she climbed the stairs to change for her shopping trip.

Veronica was pretty, but not as beautiful as her mother. She was paler than Jordan too -- almost pecan colored. She had a great sense of humor. The two of them were obviously close -- they giggled together in a way that she and Hope never had.

As they were seated in one of the trendier restaurants, Evelyn noticed how many of the patrons looked up and smiled when they saw Jordan wending her way to their table. A couple of them even reached out to touch her. Jordan took the time to smile and squeeze their hands.

"It must be hard to be so well known," Evelyn commented. "You can never just run to the store for a carton of eggs."

"Oh," Veronica said, "Mom's not like that."

"You can't be," Jordan said. "I'd never get anything done if I had to do my makeup before I left the house."

"But you look gorgeous today," Evelyn protested.

"We're shopping on the Strip. The merchants need to recognize me -- that's how I get good tables and good deals."

"Everyone wants Mom as a customer," Ronnie inserted. "If they sell it to her today, they might see it on their big screens tonight."

"Outside of Vegas, I may be a nobody. But to the locals around here, baby, I'm a star." She smiled brightly before laughing.

The waitress appeared, and Jordan ordered for all of them. When she left, Evelyn asked, "Why didn't you go for the big time? You could have been the evening news anchor for the network."

"It's all about quality of life," she sighed. "I had a shot a few years back. They were scouting me to replace Crista Andres on the morning show. But I had Ronnie to think about -- and I knew she wouldn't like New York."

"I would have adjusted," Ronnie said.

"Your seventeen-year-old self certainly didn't think so." She laughed softly and shook her head. "You had a meltdown to end all meltdowns. 'I can't leave Max! I love him so much! I'll die without him!'" she playfully mimicked her daughter's voice.

"His name was Mark."

"You hear that, Evelyn? Was. She broke up with the boy two days after I turned down the job."

"And I'll never hear the end of it," Ronnie said.

"Families have long memories," Evelyn said, thinking of her children.

"You can say that again." Ronnie smiled. "I'm glad you came along today. You should move here permanently -- I could use a friend like you. Aunt Megan is a little old to hang out with."

"I don't know if that's in the cards," Evelyn answered honestly. "I'm a media major back at school. I'd have to find a position at a local station."

"Isn't your boyfriend the new co-anchor at Mom's station? I'd say you have some pull there."

Evelyn felt the color rise to mask her normally pale face.

"Don't be embarrassed," Jordan said matter-of-factly. "Everyone gets a leg up in this business -- that's how it works."

"There are other stations in Vegas. I could look for work there instead."

"I wouldn't count any eggs in those baskets," she scoffed. "Trust me -- you want to be where Julian is. Besides, I probably don't have a lot of years left on the desk."

"Mom!" Ronnie exclaimed. "Don't talk like that."

She shrugged. "It's true. What happened to Crista Andres will happen to me eventually. No one wants to watch a woman age. It's different for men -- those aren't wrinkles, they're character. That gray hair? Makes a man look distinguished. The only thing gray hair and wrinkles do for a woman is make them look O-L-D."

Despite herself, Evelyn giggled. Ronnie joined, and pretty soon, all three of them were laughing hysterically.

#

"How was your shopping trip with the enemy?" Julian grumbled as she walked into the great room.

"Fine, thank you. Jordan is really nice, and her daughter is a sweetheart."

He looked at Evelyn queerly. "Sweetheart? Isn't that an odd thing for one woman to call another?"

Evelyn shrugged it off. "She is what she is."

"Sometimes I wonder about you, babe. You use words like a seventy-year-old woman."

"Doesn't that make me sound mature?"

He laughed before remembering he was mad at her. "You shouldn't have spent time with her," he admonished. "How are you going to feel when you take her place at the station?"

"I can't do that to her." She dropped onto the sofa next to him. "I'm sorry. This city loves her. I can't step into her shoes. People will hate me."

He put his arm around her. "You are beautiful, talented, and personable. Professor Andres picked you out of a sea of other students and called you a star."

60

Evelyn snuggled against him. "Maybe my star needs to shine somewhere else."

"I want you here, next to me." He squeezed her shoulder. "Look, I know that Andres warns media students against dating each other. She was pissed when she found out about us -- she told me to break it off when I left."

"She did? But she said we could probably find work together!"

"She was just being nice. Privately, she told me we would be each other's ruin. I think she's wrong though. We belong together. You keep me sane. You remind me of who I was before I took this job. And you're right. I have lost some of my sincerity since I moved here. With you by my side, I can be a good man. Without you...I'm just another smarmy weather guy."

"You're not qualified to do the weather," Evelyn mumbled against his chest.

"Thanks for reminding me." he tickled her ribs and she jumped.

"Hey!"

He pushed against her as he continued to tickle until she was squirming and laughing breathlessly beneath him. Pressing his weight down, he kissed her. As she caught her breath, he whispered against her ear, "I love you, Evelyn. Would you marry me?"

"What?" she gasped.

"Marry me. Be my wife. Together, we can make history."

"I still have..."

"You don't need it."

"I have to finish college," she said firmly. "I love you, Julian, but I have to be able to take care of myself."

"I'll take care of you. Look around."

She pressed both hands against his chest. "Let me up. I can't think like this."

"Maybe I don't want you to think," he said playfully.

She frowned. He moved off of her.

"Why now?" she asked.

"Because," he answered, "having you here has reminded me of how much I've missed you for the last year."

She cast her eyes forward, focusing on the view of the backyard and the pool. "Have you been faithful to me?" she asked.

"I've never told another woman that I loved her."

"That's not the answer I was looking for."

He sighed. "I know. But you aren't seeing the whole picture. I didn't have a way in. I had to play the game."

"A way in? You mean getting the reporting job wasn't enough?"

He shook his head. "You know I wanted to be on the news desk. You only get there by...making sacrifices."

"Megan?"

He nodded.

"Anyone else?"

"No. I swear. No one that mattered."

"What does that mean?" She felt the fault line in her heart begin to crack apart. The Cure could fix a lot of things, but it couldn't fix heartbreaks. Still, she couldn't blame him too much. Hadn't she slept her way to the top of an industry once upon a time? "Never mind," she said when he didn't answer. "I understand. But if I'm going to marry you, you need to be faithful to me from now on."

"I'm where I need to be, career-wise," he said confidently. "And I've never loved anyone the way I love you."

She smiled. "That's all I can really ask for, isn't it?"

#

She called Carmen that night. "I'm getting married."

"You can't do that! You still have a year left of college."

"I know. But Julian wants me here in Vegas. I'll find a way to finish. I can take internet classes if I need to."

"Does he know how old you are?"

"That doesn't matter."

"Of course it does! You're old enough to be his grandmother. As a matter of fact, you'll probably get along better with her than with him!"

Evelyn dropped onto the loveseat in their master bedroom, glad that she had waited until Julian left for work to make this call. "Don't be cruel, Carmen. You're the reason I'm in this situation in the first place. Did you really expect me to go through the next fifty years alone?"

Her sister sighed. "No," she said finally. "But I just assumed you would make a septuagenarian very happy."

"Why should I waste this body on someone old? I want someone who makes me feel sexy and wanted."

"You've had that before, haven't you?"

"No."

"What about Marty? I know for a fact that he--"

"It's not the same, Carmen. Marty only knew the older me. He loved me, yes, but when Julian looks at me, it's like he's figuring out which part he wants to devour first."

Carmen grunted. "So you want to be treated like a piece of meat."

"Listen, I just thought you should know."

"Thanks. Am I invited to the wedding?"

Evelyn hesitated before saying, "It's probably just going to be a little Justice of the Peace thing. Neither of us has a lot of friends here."

"Are you going to tell Hope and Desmond?"

"They haven't contacted me since Alan died. I don't think they care what I do, as long as I'm not in their lives."

"I guess I don't care either. I liked you better when you were older. If I had known that curing you would turn you back into..." Carmen sighed. "Have a happy life, Evelyn."

"Don't be like..." Evelyn heard the click as the line disconnected. She dropped her hands to her lap. The muted television showed her fiance smiling as he bantered back and forth with Jordan, who looked beautiful as usual.

School would start again in two weeks. She wondered what Professor Andres would advise her to do. She remembered the words Andres had written at the top of every class syllabus Evelyn had ever received from the woman: "Love is fleeting. Broadcast journalism is forever."

Chapter 5 Old Souls

Arleta hugged her as soon as she walked through the door. "Oh, my God! I thought you weren't coming back!" her roommate exclaimed.

"I had to, didn't I? I'm only one year from a degree."

"But...Vegas! A whole summer in the best city on earth!"

"I wouldn't say that. It's a dustbowl with a lot of neon signs."

"Don't give me that. My parents have been there and they say it's more fun than Disneyland."

Evelyn shrugged. "I guess I didn't see that part of the town. What did you do this summer?"

Arleta took the hint and dropped the subject, switching instead to her summer internship at some drug company located near New York City. From the sound of things, Arleta had spent a fair amount of time running errands for the scientists instead of working in the labs -- not that the girl minded. She had never seen the Big Apple before, and she took full advantage of the opportunity. She even saw Diana Mogens -- one of Evelyn's favorite actresses -- in a Broadway musical.

"That's amazing! How was the show? Was she good?"

Arleta rolled her eyes. "What do you think? She's only the best actress of the century. I wish she would make more movies."

Evelyn sat down on her bed. "I hope I get to interview her someday. That would be a dream."

"Didn't your Professor Andres interview her once?"

"Yeah...when she was doing those pre-Oscar interview shows. What a great job that must be -- interviewing the biggest stars."

"Maybe you'll be doing that someday."

"Maybe." She pulled out her phone and glanced at the screen. No calls or messages from Julian.

"What's wrong?" Arleta asked.

"Nothing."

"Nothing? Must be Julian."

"I know you don't like him, but--"

"But nothing. He's an idiot. Any guy who ignores you as much as he does would be an idiot, in my opinion."

"He asked me to marry him."

Arleta collapsed onto her own bed. "Really? Are you going to?"

Evelyn twisted the cheap silver ring he had given her as a placeholder for the real ring they were supposed to pick out together.

"Is that an engagement ring? Let me see it," Arleta demanded.

"It's just a promise ring. When I decided to come back to school--"

"I knew it! He tried to keep you there, didn't he?"

Arleta's mousiness had definitely receded over the summer. Evelyn wondered if the girl behaved like this with everyone now. "He misses me, and I miss him. But I decided that I needed to finish college more than I needed the reassurance of marriage."

Arleta frowned. "I need to pick up my class schedule. You want to come?"

"No. I think I need a nap."

"Okay. See you later." Her roommate left, pulling the door shut behind her.

Deciding that she could apologize first, Evelyn pressed the button to call Julian.

"Hello? Julian's phone," answered a female voice that sounded remarkably like Megan.

Evelyn hung up.

# # #

Evelyn scheduled an appointment with Professor Andres during the first week of classes. The marred but brilliant woman welcomed her to her office warmly. She even offered her student a cup of tea and a biscuit, an afternoon habit she claimed to have acquired during her years as a foreign correspondent stationed in Great Britain. Evelyn gladly accepted the tea, but passed on the biscuit.

"Now then," Professor Andres said as she eased into her office chair, "how may I help you, my dear?"

"Well, Professor," Evelyn began.

"Please. You are my most promising student. We spend more time together, you and me, than I do with my dog. Call me Crista."

"Okay. Crista. I need to know if you really believe I have a chance at succeeding in this business."

Crista smiled kindly and set her cup on her desk. "What a thoughtful question. Most of your fellow students simply believe in their own star quality, you know. I believe that level of confidence is brought on by the uniquely American belief that children should never have a moment of doubt about themselves. Do you know there was a time when people -- even children -- competed for prizes? Not just the so-called participation awards, but actual prizes. Contests like that were fading away when I was a child, but I remember some of them."

Evelyn remembered them as well, but she listened in silence as the woman rambled on.

"The true reason that America isn't a so-called 'super power' anymore has more to do with that than anything. We have bred the competitive spirit out of our youth." She sipped her tea, staring, with narrowed eyes, at Evelyn over the brim. "But you? You're a throwback. It's not that you won't compete -- it's that you don't want to lose the race. You're afraid you may be a donkey joining a thoroughbred's competition."

Evelyn nodded and smiled. "Precisely."

"Don't worry. You're a winner, Evelyn. If I were a betting woman, I'd put my life's savings on the line that you'll go the distance."

Thank you...Crista. You know, I nearly dropped out--"

"What?! Why would you do that?! Without a degree, it doesn't matter if you're a winner or a loser...you simply don't get the chance to run."

"A station in Las Vegas offered me a position--"

Crista laughed. "The one where Julian is working? Of course they did. They're looking for a novelty to splash across their billboards. They probably already had the tagline written: 'Love Trumps Everything' or something equally cheesy. Anything to compete with the flash of the Strip, right?"

"It was on the anchor desk. Julian and I would have been a team."

Crista frowned as she dunked her biscuit in her tea. "Wait. Isn't Jordan Meriweather his co-anchor?"

"Yes. You know her?"

Her eyebrows shot up. "Just about everyone in the business knows her. She was on track to take over my position until she put the brakes on."

"Her daughter didn't want to move."

"The only thing that trumps a career: children. I'm glad I never had any, personally. The whole world would know her name if she had taken the network desk." She sighed. "So, what made you think they would dump Jordan and replace her with you?"

"The station manager wants fresh faces."

Crista scoffed."I know that the locals are generally fickle when it comes to news anchors -- here today, gone tomorrow -- but Jordan is a fixture in that town. She's a hometown girl who has broken half a dozen scandals...everything from shoddy construction practices to lipsynching divas. She wouldn't have gone down without a fight, and she would have had a mob--" a smile played on her lips "--if not THE mob backing her play."

Evelyn nodded, agreeing with Crista's analysis of the situation. "I wouldn't want to go up against her. Not only is she a genuinely nice woman, but she is also like a rock star in that town. I went to lunch with her--"

"While you were contemplating replacing her?"

Evelyn reluctantly nodded. "But not seriously. Even though Julian was pushing for me to take the offer, I just couldn't see it."

"But you said you nearly dropped out. If not for the job, then why?"

She took a deep breath. "Julian asked me to marry him."

"Oh." The professor leaned back in her chair. "And you agreed?"

"I said yes, but after talking with my sister, I reconsidered."

"Your sister must be very persuasive to talk someone your age out of marriage. In my experience, most people under twenty-five don't take advice well." She laughed lightly. "Then again, you seem to be the exception to that rule. Are you sure you're not over forty?"

She swallowed hard and tried to laugh. "That would be a miracle, wouldn't it?"

"Damned right. I know women who would kill to look as good as you do -- and I'd be at the front of the line. Listen, Evelyn, you made the right choice. Finish your degree. After that, if you still want to marry Julian, go back to Vegas or whatever small market he's working in. You need to know that he is never going to climb any higher than he is right now. There's nothing special about him -- at least not in the broadcast journalism market. The only way he'll hit a market bigger than Vegas is with you by his side. And, quite honestly, he's a fool if he doesn't realize that."

#

After her first attempt to call Julian, Evelyn decided to wait for him to reach out to her. Professor Andres' words made her certain that he would. He needed her more than she needed him -- and Julian was no fool.

In the meantime, she focused on her studies and avoided too many distractions. More often than not, she found herself in Arleta's company. Arleta may have developed a more confident persona, but she simply wasn't a party animal. She was as focused on her studies as Evelyn was on her own.

One night, they both found themselves done with their homework at about the same time.

"There's a news program coming on that I'd like to see," Arleta said.

"You don't have to humor me. We can watch something else. Maybe something on one of the science channels?"

"No, seriously. They're reporting on one of the drugs that the company I interned for is developing. It's called Promorterem."

Evelyn sucked in a breath.

"Are you okay?"

"Fine," she lied. "Doesn't 'mort' mean death?"

"Very good!" Arleta congratulated. "I didn't know you knew Latin."

"Just a smidge."

"That's more than most people," she snorted. "I only learned what I had to for scientific purposes."

"What's the drug do?"

"Good question. All kinds of rumors were floating around the lab. I overheard a couple of the techs talking about it. They said it wasn't even really a drug. All of the funding for the project comes from some Silicon Valley guy who flies in once every few months to check on their progress. If it does what the name suggests..." She shook her head and laughed. "But that's ridiculous."

"Why?" Evelyn prompted.

"Because it sounds like it's meant to cure death! No one can do that!" She picked up the remote and flicked on the television hanging above their room's door. A few moments later, the familiar face of one of the major networks' reporters filled the screen.

"Good evening. I'm Donna Cain. On tonight's program, I will take you where no news camera has gone before -- into the belly of a pharmaceutical beast that has been fed by Mose Baxter for the last ten years. That's right" -- a picture of the reclusive tech billionaire flashed on the screen -- "that Mose Baxter. The same genius who developed app after app to make our lives easier has spent a large portion of his fortune trying to make our lives" -- Donna paused for effect -- "longer. Learn more tonight on *Modern Revelations*."

The theme music played as Evelyn glanced at her roommate. This could be bad -- very bad. No one had questioned her birthdate when she enrolled in college. Maybe they thought it was a clerical error. In any case, she had the money to pay for her tuition as well as her room and board. No college would turn away a paying student, no matter what his or her birth certificate said. Her "peers" -- her fellow students who were decades younger than she was -- had never questioned her age. They assumed she was in her late teens or early twenties, just like they were. She hoped *Modern Revelations* hadn't uncovered all of the sordid details about Promorterem.

Donna Cain filled the screen again as she led the viewers through labs and interviewed scientists and technicians about the so-called "drug." She tracked down Mr. Baxter and confronted him with allegations of genetic manipulation, which, of course, he denied. Finally, she interviewed a few young-looking people who claimed to have been treated with Promorterem. When Donna asked their ages, the woman claimed to be seventy-seven and the man said he was sixty-three. Both looked to be in their early twenties. They refused to use their real names because, they said, they wanted to protect their families. They claimed the drug had ruined their lives.

Arleta paused the show and looked at Evelyn. "What do you think?"

She shrugged. "I don't know. You?"

"I think it's all a bunch of crap," she laughed. "Let's just say for a second that there really was a drug that gave old people their youth. Wouldn't it cost...I don't know...a billion dollars? Wouldn't every Hollywood star past their prime be clamoring for it? And if you had a grandma who suddenly looked younger than your mother, you would say something, wouldn't you?"

"Maybe the drug company makes the patients sign something -- you know, a pledge of silence."

"Then why aren't these two keeping their mouths shut? And that still wouldn't stop their kids or grandkids from saying something. Why aren't they on the show to back up their elders' claims?"

"Maybe they are on later. The show's not over."

Arleta grimaced, but started the show again.

Donna interviewed the woman first. She said she had been part of a clinical trial conducted in the Northwest. She and her fellow patients had all been diagnosed with terminal cancer. Evelyn squinted at the screen, trying to imagine the woman with wrinkles and gray hair. They had probably sat in the same room more than once, since they had probably been in the same clinic. No matter how hard she tried, though, she couldn't remember the woman.

"I thought," said the woman they were calling Jane, "that I had nothing to lose. I was dying, after all. Seventy-one seemed like too few years. I wanted to grow old with my husband -- who was still in good health at the time -- and I was willing to try anything." The woman broke down in tears. "If I had known...what would happen. I never would have done this to myself."

Donna probed the woman gently. "Where is your husband today?"

"He died two years ago. Heart attack. And now I'm alone. I'll be alone for decades. Cancer was better."

The man called John was handsome, with blond hair, blue eyes, and chiselled features. He had been suffering from Lou Gehrig's disease when he was given Promorterem. "It was like a miracle from God," John said. "Within a single day, my family and I saw a difference. Suddenly, I could breathe easier. After two weeks, I felt like a teenager again. Everything, even my sex drive, was back to how it had been forty years ago. My kids were thrilled. My wife was overjoyed. For the first year after my cure, we celebrated. I spent more time with my kids and grandkids. My wife and I traveled everywhere we had ever wanted to go. But then the pension board caught wind of the fact that I was no longer sick. Unfortunately, they thought I was dead. They hired investigators and alerted the local police force that I was missing...even though I wasn't. No one would believe us, and when I contacted the pharmaceutical company, they refused to provide proof that I had been a participant in the drug trial that saved my life. Even without a body, the police arrested my wife for murder. The pension board suspended my benefits. No one will hire me because they assume I'm lying about my credentials -- I obtained a PhD in Physics back in the Twenties. I might as well be dead. Instead of dying of a terrible disease, my whole family is suffering from my terrible cure. It's a nightmare."

Donna returned to the pharmaceutical company with "Jane" and "John's" claims, where she ran into a wall of silence. All of the people who had been so eager to talk about the top-secret drug were either fired or enticed to shut up by the company. Mose Baxter wouldn't comment on either the project or his financial support of it. After hours of research and interviews, even Donna Cain refused to put into words what exactly Promorterem was. "Either," she said at the end of the show, "Mose Baxter is funding a project that will cure death or Jane and John are sharing remarkably similar delusions. On the face of it, neither seems plausible. To paraphrase the famous fictional detective Sherlock Holmes, when we eliminate the impossible, whatever remains -- however improbable -- must be the truth. If only we were able to find corroborating witnesses, perhaps we would be able to prove that Jane and John are not delusional. However, the danger seems clear: talk to anyone at your own risk. Jane and John are, at this time, both being held in psychiatric wards. Jane has no family to worry about her, and John's children refuse to speak about the situation. John's wife remains in jail pending her trial for his -- or maybe someone else's -- murder."

The screen faded to black and the credits rolled. Arleta flicked the screen off. "What do you think?"

Evelyn flipped onto her back and, pressing her palms against her abdomen, took a deep breath. "I think if I had a second chance at life, I'd do whatever I had to do to keep myself out of crazy jail, even if that meant lying about my past."

Arleta laughed. "So you think that if Jane were sane, she would have just kept quiet about the whole thing?"

"Wouldn't you?"

Arleta rolled to face Evelyn and propped herself up on one elbow. "I guess. I mean, my grandma has said to me that she'd like to start over with all the knowledge she has now." She inhaled sharply. "What if one of our classmates is actually an old man or woman? How weird would that be?"

"Yeah," Evelyn echoed, "weird."

The next day, Evelyn couldn't escape the discussions of Donna Cain's news report. It seemed that everyone had either watched the show or heard all about it. A student in one of Professor Andres's classes asked Crista what she would do if she were able to have a fresh start.

"That's easy," Crista answered with a wistful smile. "I'd go back to my old job on the network."

"Do you miss it?" called out another student.

"Terribly. There's no job like it. I envy you students -- someday soon, some of you will find yourselves in front of the television cameras bantering with your co-anchor and sharing the news with your city -- or even your country." She looked at Evelyn and winked.

Evelyn squirmed uncomfortably.

"Let's get to the lesson, shall we?"

After that class, she went to the commons and got a snack, determined to focus on her classwork and not think about the potential for disaster that seemed to be lurking around every corner. Settling into a booth, she unwrapped her sandwich and turned on her reading device.

Behind her, two frat boys were talking and laughing loudly.

"Shit," said one of them, "that's the last time I use my 'old soul' line."

"Yeah," said his buddy, "bitches be takin' that wrong now." In a high-pitched mimicking voice, he said, "Are you calling me a freak?"

Evelyn shuddered, gathered her things, and headed for her dorm room. She walked past a few groups of students talking in the lounge. In the background, a 24-hour news channel was recapping *Modern Revelations* for its viewers.

Arleta was already up in their room with one of her friends. They stopped talking when Evelyn came in. "Hey! I thought you were in class."

"My next one isn't for another hour," Evelyn mumbled.

"So, um...Evelyn. Did you know that Liz here works in Records?"

"No." She pushed her pillow against the wall and sat down on her bed.

"Yeah. And she saw that show last night."

"Hmm."

"Guess what she did this morning at work?"

Evelyn stared coldly at the girls. "Pried into other people's business?"

"No," Liz said, jutting out her chin. "I was merely protecting the interests of my peers."

"Just how old are you, Evelyn?" Arleta asked.

"How old do you think I am?" she retorted.

"Clearly, we can't trust our eyes anymore. The records say you were born in 1990. That makes you well past sixty. You're actually old enough to be my grandmother."

"What difference does it make how old I am?"

"I'll tell you what the difference is," Liz said. "The difference is you already had your chance. What makes you so special that you get another go? My grandfather died of cancer last year...no one offered him a magical cure. And I'll tell you what else -- he wouldn't have taken it anyway. He was too smart for that. Why would he want to do it all over again?'

Evelyn looked at Arleta. "Could you close the door, please?"

"Why? Do you have something to be ashamed of?" Liz asked, her voice climbing in both pitch and volume.

"No. I just want to have a civilized conversation with the two of you without the rest of the floor knowing what we're talking about."

Arleta broke eye contact with Evelyn but closed the door. "I thought you were my friend," she said quietly.

"I am. Why does my age determine whether or not we are friends?"

"How many of there are you?" Liz interrupted. "A thousand? Ten thousand?"

"I don't know. I was part of a small clinical trial for cancer patients. I didn't know what the drug would do. I only took it because my sister -- who is a doctor -- asked me to. If I had known I would be young again...I don't know if I would have taken it."

"But you probably would have, right? I mean, here you are, in college, starting back at the beginning. How screwed up was your life?"

"I don't owe you an explanation."

"What about me?" asked Arleta. "You've been passing yourself off as someone my age...don't I deserve an explanation?"

Irritation rose from the pit of Evelyn's stomach, creating a bile she hadn't tasted in years -- not since the night Alan kicked her out. "You want an explanation?" she spat. "If you had any of these other girls for a roommate, everyone on campus would call you Mouse. You timid little thing...without me, you would have run squeaking back to the backwoods farm you were raised on. I have been a goddamn fairy godmother to you for four years! And this is how you repay me?"

"I'm not a mouse!" Arleta shouted, her voice creeping into the highest octave Evelyn had ever heard from a human. "You are...unnatural! That's what you are! And everyone is going to know it!"

"Yeah!" inserted Liz, clearly anxious to be part of the mob that seemed destined to form at their doorway. "You don't belong here! You don't get to steal our futures out from under us!"

Evelyn took a deep breath. "Let's talk about this rationally." Her hands were trembling; she threaded them together to hide her fear. "What can I do to make this right?"

"Nothing!" Liz said too loudly.

Arleta shot her a silencing glance. To Evelyn, she said, "You aren't who I thought you were."

"You're not who your family thought you were," Evelyn replied. "Did you purposely mislead them?"

"I never lied to them!"

"I never lied to you. You just never asked the right questions."

"So you're saying if I had asked you what year you were born in, you would have been honest?" Arleta's eyebrow arched doubtfully.

Evelyn sighed and shook her head. "You're right. I would have told you what you expected to hear -- not the truth. But I would have had to. You saw last night what the pharmaceutical company is doing to those two people. Their lives are ruined. Unless I was willing to be dragged off to the loony bin, I had to protect their secret."

Arleta looked at Liz and shrugged. "She has a point."

"Doesn't matter. Why does she get a second chance? What makes her so special?"

"Clinical trials are like that, Liz. Maybe Evelyn had a better chance of being accepted as a patient because of her sister...maybe not. There's no way to know. But it's not her fault that she's well and your grandfather is dead."

Liz clenched her jaw.

"Thank you," Evelyn said.

Arleta shook her head. "I'll talk to you later, Liz," she said to her friend, who looked at her with disbelief.

"Are you really...?"

"We'll talk later. Don't tell anyone about this."

She shot an angry glance at Arleta but nodded before leaving the room.

"Will she keep it a secret?" Evelyn asked anxiously.

"For now. But she's not going to forget. And I don't think she should. This...drug or whatever...this is going to cause a revolution. Older generations already have an advantage over us. Now they get to reclaim their youth whenever they want it? And you know it's going to be super-expensive. No one but the rich will be able to afford it. Most insurance plans probably won't cover it. It's going to create an immortal 'ruling class.'"

Evelyn recognized those thoughts; she had them herself when she realized she was returning to her youth. She nodded. "It's a dangerous thing."

"Is it a drug?"

"Not exactly. My sister says it's like a tiny supercomputer. It was injected into me. The doctors say it corrects all of a person's cells to their most perfect condition, and then it goes inactive."

"That's crazy. It's like something out of *Star Trek*."

"Yeah."

Arleta sat down on her bed across from Evelyn. "You're going to have to leave school. Liz isn't the only student who will be outraged by this. I've already heard some pretty hateful things on campus."

Evelyn told her about the "old soul" comment she had overheard.

"That's mild. The medical science geeks are up in arms. If this thing works, our chosen careers are all but obsolete. We'll end up working at McDonald's and using our degrees for toilet paper."

Evelyn sucked in a breath. "It's not that dire, is it?"

"See? Now that's how I should have known you were old. Your vocabulary runs circles around mine -- or any other student's." She smiled. "It's actually kind of liberating to find out that you're old. I've spent four years wondering why I wasn't as mature as you are. Now it all makes sense."

Evelyn cast her eyes at the floor. "What am I going to do?"

"Maybe you should go back to Vegas and marry Julian."

"I think he's cheating on me," she confessed quietly.

"So? He's not married to you yet."

"You think it's okay to marry someone who sleeps around?"

She shrugged. "Everyone our age does it. Even I've had a few one-night stands, and I'm not exactly typical."

"This is different. He's been sleeping with his boss."

"Even less of a problem. He's doing it for career advancement, not love. Seeing as how all you old people are going to be competing for jobs with us, Julian's probably smart to use any advantage he can."

"How pragmatic of you," Evelyn said dryly.

"I'm not trying to hurt your feelings. But it's time to drop the twentieth-century mores."

"Maybe so. But I still need my degree."

"No, you really don't. The semester will be over in a month. Just don't come back."

Evelyn felt her throat close. "Where am I supposed to go?" she choked out.

"Go to Vegas. Go to your sister. Go to Hell. I really don't care anymore." With that, the girl Evelyn had spent her college career protecting dismissed her from her life.

#

"Hello?"

"Hello, Megan. Please put Julian on the line," Evelyn said.

"He's busy right now."

"I really need to talk to him."

"Listen, I like you and everything, Evelyn, but you walked away. He's fair game in my book."

"I don't really want to read a page from your book right now, Megan. I need to talk to Julian." She heard Julian say something in the background. "I know he's there. Give him the phone."

"It's her," Megan said away from the receiver.

Evelyn heard the shuffling sound of the phone being passed between hands.

"Evelyn."

"I made a mistake, Julian," she said.

"Yeah, I guess you did." His voice was cold -- almost as cold as Megan's.

"I still love you," she pushed on. This was the most important call of her life, and she couldn't let a little resistance push her off course. "I want to come back to Vegas at the end of the semester."

"I'm with Megan now."

"Yeah? Your cock must be frozen solid."

He made a noise somewhere between a grunt and a chuckle.

Encouraged, she said, "You know I can warm it up for you with one breath."

He cleared his throat. She heard his hand slide over the receiver as he said, "I'm going to take this outside, Meg. Why don't you go get ready?" She heard his shoes click against the Saltillo tile and the sound of the French door that led to the pool opening and closing. "Why now?"

"I've called a few times, actually. The ice princess always answers."

"She's not that bad, Evie."

"She's horrible."

"At least she's here."

"You know I had to come back to college, Julian. I've got to have this degree."

"Great. You needed the piece of paper. You've got one semester to go. Why would you leave now?"

She swallowed. "I miss you. And Professor Andres has agreed to let me finish my senior thesis off-campus. I only have one class that requires my attendance, but the college offers it online anyway."

"I miss you too," he admitted with a deep sigh. "But Megan thinks this is going somewhere. She sees us as a power couple -- she's a crack station manager and I'm a handsome news personality. She's already got some interest in a package deal in L.A."

"Is that what you want, Julian? Is your career more important than our love?" She knew she was selling something he might have decided he could live without, but it was the only product she had.

"I do miss you," he admitted. "But I thought we were breaking up. Obviously, I haven't been faithful."

"I understand."

"You do? Really?"

"Yes," she lied, hoping her heart would catch up with her mouth. "I might have done the same thing in your shoes."

If he knew she was lying, he didn't say. "I need to talk to Megan about this."

"Why? How is this Megan's business?"

"Geez, Evie, she's practically living with me!"

Her heart thudded with anger, but she knew she needed to hold it in. Julian was her only escape route. Going back to her sister's house meant living the life Carmen thought she should live. Stepping out on her own meant risking exposure as one of the "undead," as the news media had already jokingly begun referring to Jane, John, and a few others who had stepped forward in the last few weeks. She admired the courage of those who were willing to risk their lives to support Jane and John, but she wasn't that brave. She would keep her secret as long as she could. The venom spewed from television commentators and man-on-the-street interviews was more than enough to scare her into silence. "Okay. Just have her out before I get there. Finals are in two weeks. I'll book a ticket for the day after my last test."

They said goodbye and hung up. Evelyn looked around the room she shared with Arleta. She hadn't seen Arleta much since she issued her ultimatum; Evelyn suspected she was sleeping elsewhere in order to avoid her. She was saddened to know that she had lost Arleta's friendship, but she had no control over the situation.

Carmen called her a few days after the news program that was destroying her life aired. She had confessed the whole story to her sister, who was less than sympathetic. "You got a whole new life, and there you go making a mess of it. It's like you're physiologically unable to live a good life, Evelyn." She offered to let Evelyn come back to Portland and live with her, but Evelyn knew things would have to become impossible before she took her smug sister up on her offer.

She knew that the furor would eventually blow over. Someday, hopefully soon, Promorterem would be available through general practitioners across the country -- maybe even the world. When it was, she prayed the stigma attached to her and her fellow guinea pigs would disappear like ice melting. In the meantime, she would keep her head down and wait.

Chapter 6 Las Vegas

The Las Vegas reception wasn't quite the production it had been a few months earlier. Julian told her to call when she had her bags and he would pick her up at the curb.

After stopping a few feet shy of her, he exited his vehicle and walked toward her slowly, as if he expected her to play some sort of mean-spirited trick on him. He kissed her cheek and took her bags. She stepped into the flashy vintage Hummer. She remembered the monstrous SUVs from her childhood, though to Julian she was certain it seemed as ancient to him as a Model T did to her. When he returned to the driver's side, she asked, "A new car?"

"I needed something to get around in," he shrugged.

"Where do you get the gas for it?"

"I had it converted."

"Really?"

"Of course. Even on my salary, fifteen dollars a gallon is obscene."

She wondered how many tanks of gas he could have bought for the price of the conversion. No car made in the last ten years required gas to run, and all of them were reasonably priced. The Hummer must have cost at least a hundred grand to buy and probably another twenty to fully convert.

They hardly talked on the drive back to his house. When they parked, she walked to the back, where he handed her bag out to her. Julian's smile appeared, but soon flickered out. "I'm glad you're here."

Evelyn looked into his eyes, consciously softening her expression into something that she hoped looked like love. "Me, too." She wrapped her arms around his neck and pulled him to her so that she wouldn't have to maintain the expression for too long.

He responded, sliding his arms around her waist and sighing. "I've missed you so much."

They stood together for several moments, and Evelyn remembered the sweet boy she had fallen for when they were in college. When they broke the hug, he took her free hand and they walked into the house together.

Inside, she was surprised to see that the decor had been changed in her absence. Gone were the Mexican Day of the Dead decorations, with their brightly colored costumes and skull faces. Instead, the walls of the foyer featured two silver framed mirrors. In the center of the small space was a table on which an arrangement of fake sunflowers was balanced. She shot Julian a questioning glance.

He blushed. "If you don't like it, we can change it back. I kept my other decorations, but Megan..."

Evelyn grimaced. Of course. Megan.

She climbed the stairs to the master bedroom. It didn't appear altered at all, but Evelyn knew immediately that all of the furniture would have to go. Everywhere she looked in the room, she could see Julian and Megan fucking: on the bed, on the sofa, against the wall, on the rug. She shuddered as she walked to the closet. One item remained: a silk scarf, which was tied in a neat bow around one of the hanging bars. She felt bile rise in the back of her throat. Dropping the bag, she ran out of the closet and into the bathroom, where she promptly lost her breakfast in the toilet bowl.

Julian rushed in and found her crouched in front of the porcelain receptacle. "Are you sick? Why didn't you say so?"

"I'm fine now," she answered, resting on her knees. "Must have been a residual effect from the airplane."

"Motion sickness?"

"Yeah."

"I'll get you some water."

"Thanks."

He walked back to the sink and picked up a small glass that was sitting there. Filling it with tap water, he asked, "Are you sure you don't want to lay down for a little while?"

Another wave threatened to crest, but she swallowed it back down. "No. I'm sure I'll be fine." She took the glass from him and drank the water down in three big gulps. "We need to do something right away, though."

"What's that?"

She shifted her eyes toward the bedroom. "We need to redecorate."

At first he seemed confused, but then he nodded slowly. "Okay. I...uh...yeah. I see why you would want to do that...but I don't really...uh..."

She frowned and looked at the sea of terracotta tile around her. She glanced at the huge bath tub and saw Megan smiling evilly at her as she bounced rhythmically on top of Julian. Another wave crashed through her; the water she had just swallowed mixed with the bile and rushed out of her body and into the toilet. Tears began silently sliding down her face as she reached up and flushed her disgust away.

"We can stay in the guest room for now, okay? I promise, we will replace everything in here as soon as possible."

"Was she ever in the guest room?" Evelyn asked. She didn't look at his face; she was afraid she might be able to tell if he lied to her.

"No," he answered, "never."

#

86

Evelyn found herself unable to get comfortable in the house. It was as if Megan had left a fragment of her soul in the place; it followed her from room to room, whispering in her ear. *We made love on the table. I particularly enjoyed fucking in the pool. I gave him a blowjob in the shower.* No matter what room she was in, she pictured them together. She told herself it was ridiculous; she knew how meaningless sex could be. What Julian had done wasn't so different from her years in the porn industry -- he sold his body for a chance at a better life. And, like her, he walked away when a better opportunity presented itself. *Yes,* said the voice, *you're just a better opportunity. You are his ticket to bigger markets, just like Crista Andres said.*

After a few days of discomfort in the empty, she decided to leave the house with Julian when he went to work. "What are you going to do with yourself?" he asked as they drove toward the station's news studio.

"I don't know. Maybe I'll go shopping. Or I'll people watch on the Strip."

"You could gamble, if you want. I'll give you a couple hundred."

She nodded. "Thank you."

In the parking lot, they both exited the vehicle and, standing in front of the idling behemoth, they embraced. The warmth of his kisses was driving out the bitter cold that had been growing in her soul. As they parted, she saw the silhouette of a woman with her arms folded standing at a window on the second floor of the building.

Stepping into the driver's side of the Hummer, she waved goodbye to Julian and drove toward the Strip. When she visited the summer before, she had spent most of her time at the house, save a few trips to the colorful row of casinos and shops. Remembering the mall she had visited with Jordan and Ronnie, she circled around until she found the parking garage for the place. She wished Julian had a more practical vehicle as she hunted for a space large enough to accommodate the Hummer beast. After the better part of fifteen minutes, she found herself on the top of the parking structure. Looking around to be sure no one would be jumping out at her -- parking lots always made her nervous -- she climbed out and walked briskly toward the bank of elevators.

Once inside the mall, she relaxed. The sea of tourists swelled around her and she found herself propelled forward until she stood before a designer dress shop. She hadn't allowed herself to shop since before she was diagnosed with cancer. Though Marty had left her plenty of money, Evelyn feared that, if she lived a long life, it might run out. She admired the butter-yellow dress that draped elegantly across the mannequin in the window. It reminded her of the flapper dresses of the twentieth century.

"Beautiful, isn't it?" someone said in her ear.

Startled, she turned around to find Ronnie standing behind her. "Oh, my God! You scared me!" she said with a laugh.

Ronnie smiled broadly. "Sorry about that. What are you doing here?"

"Killing time. What about you?"

"Christmas shopping," she answered.

Evelyn had nearly forgotten the fast-approaching holiday. "That's what I should be doing as well."

Ronnie looped her arm around Evelyn's. "Let's shop together, shall we?"

Evelyn allowed the girl to lead her into the dress shop, where Ronnie investigated the price tag on the yellow dress before whistling low.

"How much?" Evelyn asked.

"Let's just say I don't love my mother quite that much."

Evelyn laughed and reached for the tag: $449. "Pricey," she commented, "but not the most expensive dress I've ever seen."

"Mom may have a terrific job, but I'm still a starving college student. My budget is about half that."

"Do you mind if I try it on?"

"I don't, but the clerk might have a heart attack."

Evelyn smiled and fingered the supple fabric. "I can afford it."

"Just how much is Julian making?"

Evelyn smiled and lifted the size-two dress off the rack as the clerk, a narrow-nosed woman with dollar signs in her eyes, approached. "I'd like to try this on, please."

The clerk looked her up and down suspiciously, but took the dress and led her toward the fitting room at the back of the store without a word.

Evelyn shot Ronnie a wink as she disappeared behind the curtain. A few minutes later, she stepped out wearing the dress. Admiring herself on the three-hundred-sixty-degree podium, she said, "Do I look like a flapper?"

Ronnie laughed. "Not exactly. For one thing, you're about a century and a half late for that era. For another, this fabric wasn't invented until a few years ago."

Evelyn spun in the shimmering dress and it gave off the warm glow of an incandescent light bulb. "This must really stand out in a nightclub."

"Yeah, it would. You'd be your own light source."

She swished her skirt and watched as the glow enveloped her legs. "I love it! I think I'll buy myself a Christmas present."

Ronnie frowned at her.

"What?"

"Nothing."

"You want one?"

"No!"

"Oh, come on...my treat."

"It's too expensive, Evelyn. I couldn't."

She stepped off the podium and took her new friend's hands. "Listen, I know this will seem odd, but I need to spend this money."

Ronnie pulled her hands away and backed up, shaking her head. "No. I don't know what your game is, but I'm not playing." She turned and headed toward the door.

"Wait," Evelyn said desperately, "I'm sorry."

"There's something not right about you," she called over her shoulder. "Stay away from me. Stay away from my mom." She took another few steps before whirling around. Her eyes were wide with realization. "You're one of them, aren't you?" she whispered.

She rushed at the girl, her hand raised to clamp over Ronnie's mouth.

Ronnie backed out of the store as the theft alarms began blaring. Evelyn stepped back as Ronnie disappeared into the crowd.

"Ma'am," said the exasperated sales clerk, "you can't leave the store in that dress."

Evelyn, sickened by how easily Ronnie had guessed her secret, only nodded and walked toward the dressing room.

"Are you purchasing it?" the clerk persisted.

Evelyn nodded. With numb fingers, she removed the garment and handed it to the clerk. She redressed and handed the clerk payment. In exchange, Evelyn received one of the shop's logoed bags. She was ten minutes behind Ronnie now, and she had no idea where the girl had gone. She walked through the mall, her eyes searching each store for her face. She didn't know what she would do when she found her -- only that she had to convince her not to spread the "wild" accusation around.

Her phone rang. She sat down on a nearby bench and answered it.

"Are you all right, Evie?" Julian asked.

"Yeah. Why?"

"You don't sound like yourself."

"I'm sorry...I guess I'm just tired."

"What are you doing?"

"I'm at the mall on the Strip."

"Christmas shopping?"

"Yeah. I guess so."

"Well, don't go overboard. Unless you're buying for me, that is."

She laughed weakly. "I won't. How's work?"

"Fine. We're done with the evening news. I'm just going to get some dinner now."

"Okay."

"Are you sure you're all right?"

"Don't worry, Julian. I'm fine." She looked up just in time to see Ronnie walk briskly past her. "I've got to go, babe. I'll see you later."

"Don't forget to pick me up."

"I won't. Love you." She ended the call and followed her prey. She waited until she was at her shoulder before saying, "Ronnie."

"Get away from me."

"Ronnie, I don't understand. What did I do?"

"You're one of them. I know you are."

"I don't know what you mean."

"Yes, you do. Stop playing stupid with me. You're..." She struggled to come up with a word to describe Evelyn. "A monster. That's what you are."

Evelyn looked as hurt as she could. "I'm not! I just wanted to do something nice for you."

Ronnie stared at her. "Why would you have that kind of money? You're a college student."

"Julian," she answered. "He takes care of me. We're practically married."

"Then why did you say...?"

"Julian has been giving me money to gamble with, but I just don't feel right about wasting it like that."

91

Ronnie blinked. "Really?"

"Of course. What did you think?"

She sighed and let out a relieved laugh. "God! Of course! I'm so stupid. It's this crazy thing with the Cure for Death. It's got us all looking for the bogeyman."

Evelyn smiled. "Yeah. Crazy, right?"

"You have to admit, though: your name is really out of vogue."

"I was named after my grandmother." Evelyn was amazed at how easily the lies slipped off her tongue. She smiled. "Friends again?"

Ronnie mirrored her expression. "Yeah. Sorry about going kinda nuts back there. I'll make it up to you."

"Did you have a good night?" Julian asked as he slid behind the driver's wheel.

Evelyn leaned over and kissed him. "Pretty good. I ran into Jordan's daughter."

"Ronnie? She seems nice. How was she?"

"Great. We did some shopping together. How was the news?"

"Same old stuff, different day. There was a shooting down by the Flamingo earlier. The killer was shouting that the victim was 'too old to live.'" He shook his head. "I don't know why everyone has gone so nuts over this Promorterem thing."

"It's just foreign, that's all."

"If you found out I was actually seventy, you'd still love me, wouldn't you?" he asked playfully.

"Of course! Why not?"

"That puts you in the minority."

"Well, I think it's ridiculous."

"I don't know," he said thoughtfully. "There's some validity to the argument that these people have already had their chance. Why should they get another shot?"

"But maybe they're just the first generation to get the chance. Maybe you'll be able to take the drug someday."

"Maybe so. We could spend eternity together, you and I." He reached across the vehicle and took her hand in his.

Chapter 7 Phoenix, Arizona – 2105

"Hope? Are you there?"

Finally, her daughter answered. "Yes, Evelyn. I'm here. What do you want?"

"The cancer is back again, sweetheart."

"So?"

"May I come see you?"

"I'm not giving you another affidavit."

"How can you say that? I'd give you one. Anytime. I gave one for Abby just a few years ago."

"You're well past a hundred. Don't you think you've lived long enough? Isn't this the third time you've been diagnosed with cancer?"

"How long is long enough, Hope?"

"You've outlived Dad by more than fifty years. And he was a good man. You don't want to die because you don't want your note to come due with the Devil."

"I'm in town. Please, Hope, let me come see you."

"Fine." She disconnected the call.

Evelyn stepped out of her car in front of her daughter's home. Its walls were shaded black; if she hadn't known better, she would have believed the building had no windows at all. She rang the bell; a moment later, her daughter opened the door. Evelyn might not have recognized her if she hadn't seen her just a few years earlier. "May I come in?"

Hope stood aside. Evelyn walked past her and into the house.

"How are you?" she asked.

"Why do you care? Worried that you'll be an affidavit short someday soon?" She looked her age -- no, she looked ten years older. She was as shriveled and shrunken as a wicked witch in a fairytale.

"What has happened to you?" she asked, her eyes wide with wonder.

"Didn't you hear? Glen took the Cure last year. He left me for a younger-looking woman. As if I needed any more proof that Promorterem is a product of Satan..."

"Don't be ridiculous. You sound like your father."

"I'd rather sound like him than be like you."

"What about Abby? How is she?"

"Terrific, I suppose. All of you have taken the mark of the Devil. I can only hope and pray that I haven't already condemned myself by giving you all affidavits." She leaned heavily on her cane as she walked ahead of Evelyn into the living room. The once-vibrant wall screens were all as black as the outside of the house. A small altar that could have been salvaged from a church sat at the far end of the living room. Hope genuflected in front of it before sitting down on the sofa.

"What is wrong with this house?" Evelyn asked.

"Nothing. It's just disconnected."

"Disconnected?"

"From the Internet," she clarified. "I don't want that evil anywhere near me. I have to keep myself as pure as possible. I want the Lord to recognize me as His own."

"Sweetheart," she said as softly as possible, "you've turned yourself into a hermit. You know the only way to get the Cure is to have ten affidavits. Cutting yourself off will make that impossible."

Smirking, Hope looked at her mother. "Don't be obtuse, Mother. I don't want the Cure. I just want to go to Heaven."

#

The list of people who might provide affidavits for Evelyn was short, and now one less name was on it. Hope refused to save her. She left her only remaining child sitting in the dim living room of her ramshackle home. As she pulled the door shut behind her, she took a deep breath of the crisp spring air and hoped this wouldn't be the last time she saw snow melt and flowers bloom.

At least Hope had given her Abigail's phone number. She dialed it.

"Hello?"

"Abby? It's Evelyn...your grandmother."

"I know who you are. Are you in town?"

"Yes."

She heard the woman sigh heavily on the other end of the line. "Have you seen Mother?"

"I'm just leaving her house."

"Did she let you inside?"

"Yes."

"That's more than she'll do for me."

"She doesn't look well, Abby."

"I know. But she won't take the Cure. Meet me at Jovan's on Central. I'll be there in five minutes."

Evelyn walked to the curb and stepped into her hovercraft. "Take me to Jovan's on Central," she said aloud.

"Instructions received," the vehicle answered.

A few minutes later, the craft was parked outside the metal-and-glass structure. She stepped out and walked to the door, where a young woman with a plain face and dark curls stood.

"Grandma," Abby said with a half-smile.

"Abby. You look great."

"Cancer is a great refresher, these days. Thanks for your affidavit."

"I'm sorry. I think that the disease might have been from my gene pool."

"That seems likely. Still...nothing like being twenty-two again. When was your last Cure? About five years ago?"

"Let's get a table."

Abby smiled at the hostess. "My party is here now."

"Of course. Let me show you to your table, Ms. Benson." She led them across the room to a table that looked out on a municipal park, handed them their menus, and retreated.

"Ms. Benson?" Evelyn queried.

"I got married just after I took the Cure last year. Sorry I didn't invite you...Mother said she wouldn't come if you did."

"I understand."

She placed the menu on the table in front of her and fold her hands on top of it. "What's wrong? You look like crap."

"Cancer again."

"I had a feeling this wasn't a social call."

"You're right. I need your help."

"What you need," she corrected, "is my affidavit."

Evelyn nodded.

"I don't have one to give you."

"But--"

"Evelyn, I would give you one if I could...I swear I would. But I have used all three of mine in the last year. I won't have another until September."

"My God...what could possibly have happened?"

My husband had a bad heart, my best friend needed a new liver, and I donated the third one to save a stranger's child. Believe me, if I could undo it now, I would. I wanted Mom to take my affidavit, but when she wouldn't...I just snapped and decided to save a kid. I didn't figure I had anyone else--"

"It's okay," Evelyn said, cutting her granddaughter off. You couldn't have known." Zeroing in on Abby's words, she asked, "Does Hope need affidavits? Is she sick?"

"Would you ladies like something to drink? Perhaps a margarita or a martini?" the waiter asked.

Both women looked up sharply.

The waiter took a step back. "I'll...um...give you both a moment," he said, retreating.

They looked at each other and laughed.

"I guess I got that expression from you," Abby said. "Mother calls it the 'eat-shit-and-die' expression."

"Another genetic pass down. It seems you received all of the worst of me."

"I don't know about that. Mother says my stubborn streak is from you."

"And that's not bad?"

"I don't think so. Look at what you've accomplished with your life: you have been immortalized on film and in history."

"Being a news reporter doesn't make me immortal."

"Young women around the country look up to you."

"And young men watch my skinflicks."

Her granddaughter smiled gently. "Be kinder to yourself. You have an amazing legacy. You have lived the longest life of any of us so far. Most people can't hack it, you know. I counsel people every day who are struggling with the gift of life. Three in ten suicides these days are recipients of the Cure. At least you knew enough to start life over when you received your first dose."

"What choice did I have? If I hadn't started over, I would have had to lock myself away."

"But it was a blessing, wasn't it? You could have been dead more than fifty years ago. Instead, you are still going strong."

"Not so strong anymore. If you live long enough, you will eventually lose everyone and everything you love."

"Then you should find new people and things to care about."

"What's the point now? I'll be dead by summer."

Abby reached across the table and grasped her grandmother's hand. "No. You won't. I'm certain you'll be fine. And I'll have an affidavit to give you in the fall. In the meantime, why don't you come and stay with my husband and me? You'll love Howard. He's such a sweet man."

"I couldn't impose on you two. You're practically newlyweds, and I know from experience that having in-laws hanging about is rough on a marriage."

"Don't be ridiculous. Howard and I have been together for ten years. We only got married because he took the Cure, which reversed his vasectomy. We wanted any children we have to be legitimate."

"You're seriously considering kids? I thought you never wanted any. Besides, you're in your sixties now, and I know the Cure doesn't replenish a woman's fertility."

"I had some of my eggs frozen when I reached forty -- just in case. It's a good thing I did. Hitting sixty-five tends to mellow one's positions on subjects such as descendants," she said, shrugging.

"What about your mother? Is she ill?"

"She has a heart condition that will eventually kill her, but she says she wants to go out 'the natural way.'"

The waiter cautiously stepped to their table again and cleared his throat. "Ladies, are you ready to order?"

"Yes," they said in unison.

#

When her granddaughter was gone, Evelyn sat in her car and made a note to check back with Abigail in September. Though she feared she wouldn't survive that long, it was good to know that her granddaughter would help her if she could. She looked up Howard Benson on her tablet and discovered that he was a prominent politician who had served as a senator for more than sixty years. She thought his name had sounded familiar. A little more research showed that he had once been vehemently against the Cure and had voted for many of the ageist policies put in place in the 2050s. She laughed softly, wondering if Abby had been the one who changed his mind.

She made a list of others she could ask for affidavits from, then she ordered the names from most to least likely. Her next stop would be Beverly Hills.

Chapter 8 New York City -- 2092

"We're so glad you came in to read for the evening news desk," said the producer with his slicked-back black hair. It was so hard to tell these days if a person was truly young or just someone who had taken the Cure. This particular network executive appeared to be about forty, but, unless he was seriously into vintage clothing, his suit put him closer to the ninety mark. On top of that, she knew that most people in broadcasting didn't surrender their jobs easily. For a forty-year-old to be in a position of power at a network was nearly unheard of.

"Thank you for inviting me in, Mr. Ayala. I appreciate the opportunity."

He nodded. "You're well thought of in the news community. Your years on the L.A. morning show have not gone unnoticed."

"That's good to know." She had been working as the lead hostess on *Good Day, L.A.* for the better part of thirty years. About ten years before -- right around the time her wrinkles started to catch up with her -- another bout of cancer had been addressed with a dose of Promorterem. The weathergirl had told her how lucky she was. Evelyn didn't feel fortunate, but she was nearly ninety by then. She had lived through the worst of the ageist riots by "passing" -- using Julian as her unwitting shield against the accusations. When she was finally exposed...well, she felt decidedly unlucky.

"You're only up against one other person, so just relax and read the news. You've got a fifty-fifty shot." Ayala smiled and winked at her.

The story was an old one, obviously from the Third World War. "Today in London, thousands have died in the worst chemical attack yet." She recognized the event -- Desmond, Leah, and their children had died there. Even as she continued to read the horrifying details, she felt tears begin to roll down her cheeks. "The canisters containing the chemical agent were placed throughout the city in public trash bins and activated remotely, according to British authorities. No country has claimed responsibility for the attack at this time." No nation ever claimed responsibility. Authorities eventually decided it was the work of anti-Cure activists, because they were the most vocal about the need for population control. "King George is expected to address his subjects and the allied nations within the next two hours." King George, who at that time had only recently ascended the throne after his father died unexpectedly in a helicopter crash, was ill-prepared to lead the country, despite being nearly seventy years old at the time. His speech, which was meant to be rousing, led to the revolt that had been predicted more than a century before and postponed by the dynamic King William, who had been beloved by his countrymen. King George was imprisoned while his mother was smuggled out of the country. All but one of her children -- a young princess born after the royal couple took the Cure -- were hunted down and assassinated.

The producer cleared his throat; Evelyn stopped reading. "Are you aware that you are crying, Miss Bryant?"

She closed her eyes for a moment. When she opened them, the TelePrompTer was thankfully blank. "I'm sorry. That one was a little close to home for me. One of my children --"

"Yes," he said pointedly, "we know. I'm sure you know how important it is for a news anchor to be able to project calmness in the midst of calamity."

She nodded. "I could do that with any other story. But my son --"

He held up one hand to stop her. "You're an amazing hostess for the Los Angeles morning show. No one will ever be able to top you. But I don't think you're, as they say, ready for primetime. Thank you for coming in."

Standing up on shaky legs, she walked as calmly as possible from the room, pulling the door shut behind her. Sitting a few feet away was a young woman who looked familiar. Evelyn gulped a few breaths.

"Are you all right, Evelyn?" It was the sound of her inner voice -- the tone, inflection, and even the pitch.

"Crista?" she said aloud.

"Yes. In the flesh."

Evelyn allowed herself to slide to the ground and look at the young woman seated nearby. "You're reading for the news desk?"

"Yes. I would imagine they will be calling me in momentarily." She reached her hand out and Evelyn took it gratefully. "What happened in there?"

"He asked me to read an old newspiece. Something that impacted my life."

"What did I tell you kids about letting your emotions show? You can never do that. Box it up!"

"I know. Any other piece and I would have been fine."

Crista squeezed her fingers. "Good luck to them if they've been looking for something that will make me cry. I could report on my own death and remain dry eyed." She smiled. "The miracles of modern medicine, am I right?"

Evelyn had heard whispers about different elective surgeries offered in private hospitals. The men and women who had once trained to be lifesavers were now body modifiers, providing everything from media implants to tear-duct control switches. She had been horrified by the idea...a sure sign that she had outlived her era. Evelyn pushed herself to a standing position and said, "Good luck in there, Crista."

"Thanks...but I've never needed it before. It was good to see you."

Chapter 9 Las Vegas -- 2050s

"Thank you for inviting us," Evelyn said as Jordan stepped aside. She and Julian walked into the well-appointed corner apartment in what was once the hippest casino on the Strip. Unlike most casinos that outlive their cachet, this one had been repurposed as a residential building with a large number of restaurants and shops filling what had once been the casino floor. The locals coveted the amazing views and compact, well-planned designs of what had once been hotel suites. Jordan's place was a two-bedroom unit with a wraparound balcony. The furniture was mid-Twentieth-century Modern with a heavy emphasis on Scandinavian design -- lots of blond woods and neon colors. "Your apartment is beautiful!" Evelyn said, awestruck.

"Thank you," she beamed. "Ronnie decorated it. You know she's in college on an art scholarship, don't you?"

"You've mentioned it," Julian answered.

One of the balcony doors slid open and Megan oozed into the room. The man who followed behind her looked like a network suit -- he had that self-important air about him that Evelyn remembered from the cocktail party nearly a year before. "Good...you made it," she said, blowing Julian a kiss. "I was beginning to think Bobby and I were going to be the only guests."

The man smiled indulgently at Megan's back before walking toward Julian with an outstretched arm. "Robert Grimes. Pleased to meet you."

"Julian Harris. And this is my fiancee, Evelyn Bryant."

"I know all about you, son. You're a hot commodity. But Megan never mentioned that you were engaged." Bobby was frowning.

"Not to worry, Bobby," Megan said, placing one hand on the man's back. "Miss Evie here is angling for a career in broadcast journalism. In fact, I think she just graduated from college. Am I right?"

Evelyn nodded while trying to keep herself from grimacing at Megan's use of her nickname. "Yes. Just this week, actually."

"Fantastic," Bobby said, stretching the word out in a way that suggested sarcasm.

"Crista Andres predicted that she would be a network star," Julian inserted.

"Crista Andres? The same Andres who was on the network news desk a few years back?"

"The same. She's the head of the Media Department where we attended school."

Bobby whistled low. "Now that's impressive. She was quite a talent before her face got messed up. Being slashed by a crazed fan is a career ender, no matter how good you are." He squinted slightly and tilted his head away from her. "You have the looks, that's for sure. Question is, do you have a voice?"

"Smooth as silk," said Jordan, who was sliding the main dish onto the table. "She's got the chops, Bobby. This girl will be a star. Dinner's ready."

The four of them moved to the table. Jordan slid into the chair at the head while each couple took a side.

"Where is Ronnie?" Evelyn asked.

"Studying for a final. She sends her regards. Julian, would you mind serving?"

"Not at all," he said, standing to carve the stuffed pork loin.

"What are your plans, Evelyn?" Bobby asked.

"I'm not sure what you mean."

"You've graduated...are you applying for jobs?"

"Not yet," Julian answered for her.

"Actually," she said, "I have applied in a few markets."

Julian's knife hesitated mid-slice. "I thought you were going to take it easy this summer."

"There's a lot of competition out there. I might not even get an interview for months."

"I wouldn't count on that," Bobby said. "Your news-reading demo will probably get you through the door easily. You've got a good look and a great voice."

"Told you so," Jordan said as Julian deposited a slice of meat on her plate.

"We would really prefer to work together," Julian said.

Jordan laughed. "Dreamer."

"I didn't mean here," Julian hastened to say. "I was hoping we could take a team desk in another market."

"That might mean a step backward for you," Bobby warned.

"I'm willing to do whatever it takes for us to work in the same location."

Jordan shook her head. "Don't base your career decisions on your love life." As an afterthought, she looked at Evelyn. "Sorry."

"Not at all. I agree."

"There's a reason most newscasters marry outside of the business," Bobby said. "Long-distance relationships are hard. They're even harder when the chances of being together are practically nil."

Finished with his carving duties, Julian sat down with a thump. "What is this, an intervention?"

"Not at all," Megan said. "I believe in you two crazy kids. I still think we can sell you as a team."

"Let's talk about something else, shall we?" Jordan suggested as she passed the green beans to Megan. "What do you all think of Mose Baxter's announcement?"

Evelyn picked up her water and, suddenly parched, gulped half of it down.

"You mean about the Cure for Death?" Bobby laughed.

Jordan rolled her eyes. "Has he said anything else lately that's been in the news?"

Bobby ignored her jab. "I think it's ridiculous. It's like saying that he's created the perfect woman...which, by the way, he claimed to have done about two decades ago."

"Oh, yeah!" Julian laughed. "The Fembot -- a living doll. That was the tagline, right?"

Bobby nodded. "Remember the commercials? The beautiful-but-blank-expressioned woman who brought the man his beer, washed his clothes, and submitted to his every whim?"

"My dad wanted one so badly I thought he was going to sell the family car. Mom put her foot down, though."

"Baxter really missed the boat on that one," Megan said. "My dad bought one and named her Nancy. She was creepy as hell. When she walked, you could hear the gears turning. She was supposed to learn what pleased her owner and develop a personality. None of us could get used to talking to her, though, and eventually she ended up in a corner of the basement."

"Your mom was okay with having one in the house?"

Megan shook her head. "Mom was dead by then. Dad thought Nancy would make a good replacement for her."

"That's awful," Jordan said. "So, Bobby...you think this is just another misfire on Baxter's part?"

"I think the guy was too heavily influenced by science fiction as a kid. There's no way that a nanocomputer can cure every disease known to man. It's just ridiculous."

"I don't know about that," Julian said. "Think of all the things that used to be science fiction. Just because consumers found Fembots disturbing doesn't change the fact that androids exist. And before the submarine and airplane were invented, they were considered science fiction, too."

"You're being awfully quiet, Evelyn. What do you think?" Jordan asked.

"I think it's possible," she answered quietly.

"Why? What convinced you?"

"I don't know...I just think... like Julian said. Things that used to be the stuff of science fiction are now everyday objects in human lives. Maybe the real geniuses are the writers who come up with this stuff and inspire people to make them real."

Everyone laughed.

"That's one for the books," Bobby said. "Maybe we're all just characters in a novel."

"It's no more unlikely than the scientific theory that we're actually just a computer simulation of life." Julian squeezed her hand under the table.

"Like that *Sims* game?"

"Exactly," Evelyn said, warming to the subject. "Maybe we're actually an advanced version of that game."

"So you're saying we're a world within a world."

"Within a hundred worlds, potentially. How would we know?"

Megan pushed away her plate. "Suddenly, I'm not so hungry."

"Are you all right?" Jordan asked.

"The table conversation tonight is a little disturbing. Alternate realities? Science fiction becoming reality? Ugh."

"Not really a fan of the genre?" Evelyn asked, bemused.

"You aren't thinking through the consequences of something like the Cure. What about population control? If no one is dying, how will we make room for children? Will children become a luxury item? Will they become obsolete? And what about jobs? If skilled but aged workers can suddenly regain their youth, what's to stop them from keeping their jobs indefinitely? This 'cure' could really be the death knell of our society. What about prisoners? Will they be able to get the cure too? Since most states don't have the death penalty anymore, will it become possible for someone sentenced to a hundred years or more to actually serve their time and be released? Do we really want someone who has spent more than a lifetime in the system to get out of jail with all the vitality of a twenty year old?"

The table was silent as the other four processed Megan's concerns. Finally, Julian said, "It won't come to that. We'll come up with a way to regulate it that will make sense."

Megan laughed bitterly. "Yeah...the government is so good at that shit." She turned to Bobby. "Will you drive me home, please? I'm really not feeling well at all."

"Of course."

"I'm sorry, Jordan. I don't mean to break up the dinner party, but I think I might be coming down with something." Megan really did look as if she were physically ill.

"Don't worry about it. Get some rest. And don't go to the studio tomorrow if you're sick. We can survive a single day without you."

Megan smiled wanly. "Yes...but can our fearless station manager?"

After Bobby and Megan left, Jordan, Julian, and Evelyn retired to the red, circular conversation pit that sat in the corner of the apartment, overlooking the Strip in all its glory.

"Thanks for dinner," Julian said. "It was excellent."

"Thanks for coming. I know this can't have been a completely comfortable evening for either of you, but I really thought Evelyn would benefit from meeting Bobby."

"I appreciate that," Evelyn said.

"I don't," Julian countered with a grimace.

"You know as well as I do that there are no on-air openings in the valley." Jordan pulled her legs onto the sofa and leaned sideways against the back of the upholstered cushions.

Evelyn admired the comfortable confidence Jordan exuded. She mirrored her position and reached out to touch Julian's hand. "It's not that I want to leave, babe. I just want to work."

He sighed and squeezed her fingers affectionately. "I know. But give Megan a chance to work her magic. She has a lot of contacts beyond Vegas. She might find us a place where we can work as a team."

Jordan's eyes drifted to the windows.

"Are you all right?" Evelyn asked.

"Fine. I'm just thinking about the Cure again. You're both so young...you probably can't even imagine what you'd do with another lifetime."

"And you can? You're only in your forties!" Julian chuckled.

"Believe me, sweetie, nearly fifty years is plenty of time to harvest regrets." She sighed. "I should have taken the network anchor job a few years ago. An opportunity like that only comes once in a lifetime."

"But you did what was right for your daughter," Evelyn said, thinking of Hope and Desmond for the first time in months.

"I'd like to think so," she sighed, "but she could have studied art a thousand different places. I should have pushed her to shoot for something higher than UNLV. I wasn't exactly a role model when it came to reaching for her dreams."

The door opened and Ronnie appeared. "Mom! I'm home!" she called as she locked the door behind her. "Oh. Sorry. I thought maybe the party would be over by now. Where's Aunt Megan?"

"She wasn't feeling well." Jordan looked pointedly at the clock. "Nine o'clock? You thought everyone would be gone this early?"

She shrugged. "You're old. Aren't you supposed to be in bed by now?" She was edging her way around the room.

"What a smartass you are! You must get that from me," Jordan joked.

"I've still got some studying to do, so could you all hold it down in here? I'll see you in the morning, Mom. Love you."

"Okay. Good night, my little antisocial lovebug."

"Mom!" The tone was a cross between a whine and a warning. Her bedroom door closing punctuated it perfectly.

Jordan laughed softly. "She loves that nickname as long as no one else is around to hear it."

"I thought you and Ronnie were friends," Julian said to Evelyn.

"More of acquaintances, really." Evelyn shifted on the sofa slightly.

"That's too bad," Jordan noted. "I was really hoping you and she would become fast friends. I think she could learn a lot from your determination."

"I guess I'm unusual that way," Evelyn conceded. "Determination in someone my age is more of an anomaly than the norm. But I wouldn't worry. If she's studying something she loves, she will eventually find the drive to have a career that satisfies her."

"Well said." Jordan stretched and stood up. "I think I'm going to have some more wine. Would either of you--?"

"No, thank you, Jordan. I think Evie and I should get going. Thank you for inviting us tonight though. We had a lovely time." Julian stood and held out a hand to help Evelyn to her feet.

"Yes, thank you very much. The dinner was delicious, and the conversation was even better," Evelyn grinned as she took Julian's hand.

"It's so nice to see a young couple so well suited to one another," Jordan said. "You know what? Don't listen to me. Love is more important than fame or fortune. Life shouldn't be all about work."

"You're drunk," Julian said.

"Why do you say that?"

"Because you aren't naturally sentimental."

Jordan laughed. "Yeah, maybe you're right. But I'm not kidding."

Evelyn hugged her hostess. "We'll see you soon."

"I'll see him tomorrow night. But don't be a stranger. We should take another shopping trip next week. What do you say?"

"Of course! Sounds like fun."

"And if you need a reference for any of your job applications, you can definitely use me."

# # #

When the phone rang early one morning a few weeks later, Julian rolled over to answer it.

Evelyn, still in that post-sleep haze, listened as her fiance uh-huhed and one-worded his way through a brief conversation. When he hung up the phone and looked at Evelyn, his eyes were flooded with tears.

"Who was that?" she asked.

"Megan. Jordan...she died, Evie."

"What do you mean? She was fine last night, right?"

He shrugged. "She seemed all right."

"Then what happened?"

"Megan says she jumped."

"From her condo?"

He nodded.

"Oh, my God...why would she do that?"

"No one knows. She didn't leave a note."

# # #

Julian reported Jordan's death somberly, but without tears. The station had a memorial reel ready to go --

113

apparently, this was standard practice for them. The tape had been updated at the end of December, so they only had to add a few finishing touches to it -- like her final signoff the night before.

As Evelyn watched it, she tried to see signs of depression in her almost-friend. She couldn't detect anything out of the ordinary. It was puzzling: why would she kill herself? She had a secure position and was beloved by the public. She and Ronnie had an exceptionally close relationship. She didn't seem lonely; in fact, she seemed satisfied with life. And she didn't leave a note.

Evelyn pulled out her tablet and searched "suicide notes." She hoped to find something that told her suicides without notes were common. What she found instead were the last words of thousands of strangers. Some of them were well-reasoned and clear; others were rambling and incoherent. All of the notes filled her with despair. She turned off the device and slid it onto the glass coffee table in front of her.

The bedroom was fully redecorated now, with light-blue sofas, glass tables, and surrealist art that used elements of nature to stand in for humans and the machines they created. The bedroom was once more her favorite room in the house. She lay down across the length of the sofa to wait for Julian to return home.

She must have slept, because the sound of the front door closing seemed to come too soon. "Julian?" she called out as loudly as she could without actually sitting up.

No one answered, but she heard the familiar sound of his gait against the Saltillo tile of the foyer. A few moments later, she heard him climbing the stairs.

She sat up and stretched.

"There you are," he said as he came through the double doors of the bedroom. "I expected to find you in the pool."

"I didn't feel like swimming tonight. How was everyone at the station?"

"Tonight wasn't a great night," he sighed. "But we have to soldier on, right?" He fell into the couch next to her. "Megan says you should get your audition tape into the studio right away."

Evelyn's stomach turned. "I can't do that."

"Of course you can. Someone has to take Jordan's spot...it may as well be you. I think that's what she would have wanted."

"I wouldn't feel right about sitting in her chair."

"Technically, it was never her chair. The whole set belongs to the station."

"You know what I mean."

"It's just a formality, babe. Megan as good as told me that she and the station manager want you as the co-anchor. As sad as this situation is, in some ways it's like a dream come true. You and I get to work together and we don't even have to sell the house."

"I guess you're right."

"Of course I'm right." He wrapped an arm around her shoulders and squeezed her close to him. "We're going to be amazing...like Leno and Letterman."

"They weren't newsmen; they were talk-show hosts."

"But what a team!"

"They were competitors."

"Everyone is a competitor against everyone else. But we'll still be amazing." He stood and stretched. "I'm going to take a shower. Wanna come with me? I'll make it worth your time." He waggled his eyebrows at her playfully.

"I don't think so. I'm pretty tired. I think I'll go to bed."

His face dropped. "Oh. Okay. I'll be there in a little while." He walked into the bathroom.

Evelyn took a deep breath and wondered if she should be crying. No tears came. She stripped out of her clothes and climbed between the sheets.

#

The funeral a few days later was the biggest one Evelyn had ever seen. One of the casinos hosted the actual service, which was held in their largest venue -- one that was normally used by a long-running Cirque du Soleil show. Large screens to either side of the podium displayed the mourners in quadruple their normal sizes, like a funhouse mirror meant to exaggerate despair.

Ronnie was the first to speak. She talked about how Jordan had always been there for her -- how she had always put her daughter's best interests ahead of her own. The station manager followed her with a tribute to Jordan's remarkable work ethic and genuine love of the Las Vegas community. A parade of also-knowns passed by, each one remembering some small thing Jordan did or said to make their lives better. At last, Julian stood and read a poem that Megan had suggested would be a good way to end the service. He seemed to tear up as he read the words; he even managed to make his voice crack just enough to be convincing. Evelyn wondered if he had missed his calling as an actor. At home, he was already cracking distasteful jokes about the dead woman and insisting that Evelyn see the positive result of Jordan's decision.

Like everyone in Las Vegas, Jordan's body was cremated. The city had long ago decided that cemeteries were a waste of resources. Her ashes would be interred in the city's Wall of Fame, a memorial that stretched along Tropicana Boulevard. (As it happened, she was placed on top of a recently deceased comedian and next to a famous transvestite, both of whom had enjoyed long careers in the entertainment mecca.)

Evelyn made an effort to seek out Ronnie and offer her condolences.

"I'm sure you're heartbroken," she sneered.

"I really liked your mom. She was so nice to me."

"She liked you as well, despite my warnings."

"What did I do to you?"

Ronnie pulled her into a corner. "I know what you are, Evelyn. I know you're one of the old souls."

"I already told you you're wrong about that."

"I didn't believe you, so I did a little research. You should really look into covering up that trail. You were born in the twentieth century. You're well into your sixties now, aren't you? Looking good, grandma." She narrowed her eyes. "You're a monster."

"I'm not! I'm just a regular person trying to get through life the best I can."

She shook her head slowly. "You're delusional. Stay away from me."

Julian appeared over Ronnie's shoulder. "Everything all right over here?"

Ronnie spun around to look at him. "And how old are you? Seventy? Eighty?"

Julian, puzzled, looked at her blankly.

"Never mind. I'm sure you're just a 'regular person' too. You know what? I should just be glad that you're all out of my life now." She turned on her heel and walked away.

"What was all that about?"

"She's got it in her head that we're old-soulers."

"That's bizarre. I mean, what are the chances that one of us would be, let alone two?"

Evelyn took his arm and smiled brightly. "I'm hungry. Let's go to the buffet."

#

Megan called her into the station a week later. Evelyn dressed carefully as she rehearsed her answers to the questions she expected Megan to ask. Giving herself a once-over in the bathroom's full-length mirror, she thought the navy-blue pantsuit might be a little authoritative. However, her other options seemed too frivolous for an interview. "Thank you so much for seeing me, Megan," she said in her sweetest voice. Good enough, she decided.

"Are you ready?" Julian called from the foyer. "We're going to be late."

Evelyn walked swiftly down the stairs. "Sorry. I just want everything to be right."

He squeezed her around the waist. "It will be. You can't fail."

They drove to the studio with music playing on the Hummer's stereo. She was glad that Julian didn't expect her to keep up her side of a conversation; she was too nervous for that. At the building's door, he put his hands on her hips and gave her a chaste kiss. "You're going to be great. Relax." He opened the door for her and pointed her toward Megan's office. "See you later."

"Thanks, babe. Have a good night." She turned in the direction he had indicated. No one was sitting at the massive reception desk, but Evelyn wasn't surprised by that. Julian had told her that the receptionist was a bit flighty and tended to wander away from her post on a regular basis. Evelyn walked down the hall until she came to the door with Megan's name on it. She knocked twice and waited.

"Come in!" called Megan.

Evelyn pushed open the door and found Julian's ex-lover, her fire-engine red lipstick perfectly applied even though it was after four in the afternoon, sitting behind a huge antique desk.

"Ah! You made it! I wasn't sure you would come."

"Thank you for seeing me, Megan," Evelyn replied.

"Come in and have a seat. We need to talk."

She followed Megan's instructions and soon found herself in a comfortable chair across the desk from her erstwhile nemesis.

"Comfortable?"

"Yes, thank you."

"Would you like a bottle of water?"

Evelyn hesitated.

"Don't worry so much. This is really just a formality."

"Yes, I would, please." She let out a breath she hadn't realized she was holding.

Megan opened a small refrigerator behind her and handed the cold bottle across the desk. She took a second one and opened it for herself. "I know you and I have had our differences, but I'm not one to hold grudges. What I said the first time I met you still stands: you and Julian would make a perfect team. You both appear young and attractive, and you have natural chemistry." She took a swig of water. "I don't know if Julian is aware, but the numbers for our station have been in decline ever since he took the co-anchor chair. We think the problem was that Jordan and Julian had zero chemistry. In fact, there have been some downright awkward moments since he started. Even though Jordan was beloved by the city, the fact remains that even her most faithful followers were getting ready to change the channel. With her out of the way--"

"The woman died, Megan. Don't you think you should be a little more...human?"

"She was becoming a liability." She flashed an irritated glance at Evelyn. "Either Julian or Jordan was going down the road. I was fighting for Julian, of course...this just made the decision a little easier on everyone."

"I just find it so hard to believe that someone as successful as Jordan would kill herself. It doesn't make sense."

"I have found very little in this world does. For instance, is it logical that I'm sitting across from a nearly seventy-year-old woman who looks better than I do?"

Evelyn breath escaped her and her eyes widened.

"Don't act so surprised," Megan said, rolling her eyes. "You have done absolutely nothing to hide your birthdate.

Perhaps you assumed that everyone would think it was a clerical error -- after all, you look like you are in your early twenties. Unfortunately, the fact that the Promorterem is now acknowledged to exist makes the 'clerical error' look increasingly unlikely. Especially since I was easily able to track down the details of your previous life."

"Please," Evelyn begged, "don't tell Julian."

"I don't intend to. I'm going to make you the best deal you'll ever get. Jordan was costing this station a small fortune. She'd been here forever, and she was a master at contract negotiations. With the ratings falling, she was becoming a huge liability." She scribbled something on a piece of paper and pushed it across the table. "That's the highest I can go on salary for you -- and that's with a five-year contract. However, as a...let's call it a signing bonus...I'm going to make your past disappear. Your new birth year will be 2032."

She blinked. Picking up the paper, she saw a salary that Julian would have laughed at -- she knew the station was paying him half again as much. "And if I refuse?"

Megan smiled. "Good luck finding a job anywhere on the planet, let alone Las Vegas. And say goodbye to your yummy boyfriend. I'm thinking he's not into old women -- I barely made the cut."

Evelyn sighed. "You've got me between a rock and a hard place."

"See? Your speech patterns are so quaint, it's amazing no one else has figured out you're old enough to be a grandmother."

She grimaced. "When do I start?"

"Why not tonight?"

"Are you kidding? I'm not dressed for--"

"Not to worry," Megan cut in. We have plenty of wardrobe selections and, of course, we have a stylist on hand to make you look your best. All you need to do is sign on the line." She slid a packet of papers across the desk.

Evelyn wondered briefly if she should be signing in blood; after all, this seemed like a contract with the Devil herself.

# # #

"Good evening, Las Vegas. I'm Julian Harris."

"And I'm Evelyn Bryant. Thank you for joining us."

"And now, tonight's news..."

Evelyn could see Megan on the other side of the cameras as Julian read the first story. She smiled when she saw Evelyn looking at her. Evelyn shuddered, but didn't miss her cue.

She and Julian had been reading the news together for nearly six months. The station was once again at the top of the heap in the market, and they passed at least three billboards with their faces on them as they drove to and from the station. It was safe to say that they were the most popular newscasters in Nevada -- and that was a good thing.

When the director signaled for the first commercial, Evelyn finished reading her news item and finished with a "We'll be right back after these messages."

Megan crossed in front of the camera to the desk. "How are you two doing tonight?" she asked.

"Great, as usual," Julian said, smiling.

"Fine," Evelyn answered.

"Good. Are we all set on the special segment, Julian?"

"What segment?" Evelyn asked.

"Never you mind. This is Julian's thing."

"Julian?"

"It's nothing," he said, touching her arm. "Relax."

"Ten seconds, Megan," the director said.

"Thanks, Joe. See you two after the show." She walked out of the frame as the cameraman said, "In five, four." He counted the last three down silently.

"Welcome back," Julian said. "As some of you may have figured out by now, Evelyn Bryant isn't just my co-anchor. She is, in fact, the love of my life."

Evelyn sucked in a breath. The station had been playing up the love connection on the billboards, but they had kept it out of the newscasts -- until that night.

Julian stood and walked around the side of the desk, where he kneeled and pulled a ring box from his jacket. "Evelyn, I can't imagine spending my life without you. Would you do me the honor of becoming my wife?"

Evelyn glanced at the camera and nodded. The studio exploded with cheers and applause as Julian slid the engagement ring on her finger.

Evelyn wanted a quick, quiet ceremony at one of the small chapels that dotted Las Vegas, but Evelyn wasn't in charge of her wedding to Julian -- Megan was. The station booked and paid for the most lavish package available at one of the Strip's newest and most beautiful resorts: the Hagia Sofia. The facade was made to look exactly like the world-famous church turned mosque, but the interior was everything the religious icon wasn't: a decadent swirl of gambling, restaurants, and art, all with a distinctly Arabian flavor. Each of the four spires offered a private suite at the top, which were rumored to be the most extravagantly decorated rooms in the city. Because Evelyn and Julian were the top news team in the city (and Megan was remarkably persuasive), the hotel manager comped them two nights in one of the spires.

The chapel was housed at the back of the massive building and featured huge windows that looked out on a garden featuring plants native to the Turkish peninsula. The walls were painted with traditional Muslim patterns and the benches were hand carved by Ankaran artisans.

"What do you think?" Megan asked after she, Julian, and Evelyn finished taking the grand tour. Not waiting for an answer, she gushed, "This place is absolutely amazing. And the hotel manager is more than happy to have us film the entire event!"

"Is all this really necessary?" Evelyn asked as she looked around at the garish opulence of the place. "I just wanted--"

"This isn't about what you want," Megan said sharply. "You two are famous. The world wants to see you two kids get hitched!"

"The world?" Evelyn scoffed. "We're Las Vegas newscasters, not movie stars."

"But the whole world loves Vegas. Did you know that clips of Julian's proposal actually made the national news shows?"

Evelyn rolled her eyes. "What do you think, Julian?"

"If the station is paying for it, who are we to say no?"

She looked at her fiance with a furrowed brow. "I thought you liked the idea of a chapel wedding."

"This is a chapel, Evie."

"You know what I meant!"

"Evie...we're celebrities! People want to see us get married so that they can celebrate with us. And they expect us to get married in a...well, showier way than they would."

"I should have known you'd already drunk the Kool-Aid," she muttered. More loudly, she said, "I only have a few people to invite. My side of the 'chapel' will look pretty empty."

"No worries," Megan said with a shrug. "We're going to offer your fans a chance to attend. We'll just put them all on your side."

"Strangers? You want us to have strangers attend our wedding?!"

Julian frowned. Megan took her arm and pulled her away, saying over her shoulder, "We'll just be a moment, Jules." When they were far enough away that Megan thought they were out of earshot, she hissed, "Listen, sister...if you don't go along with this, your secret is going to become public."

"Don't threaten me."

"Threaten you? How can I threaten something I own? And don't think for one moment that I don't own you...your precious career is in my hands. I can either propel you to the top or crush you into dust."

Evelyn swallowed down her anger. "Okay. I get it. This isn't our wedding...it's your propaganda piece."

"No," Megan said, smiling sweetly, "it's both."

The weekend before the wedding, the male members of the crew threw Julian a bachelor party at the station. They rushed Evelyn and all of the other women out as soon as the last newscast of the day was over. Evelyn, who had experienced her share of bachelorette events in her lifetime, was actually thrilled that she didn't have an entourage of women begging to party with her. She went home and curled up under the silver-blue comforter in the master bedroom. She flipped around the channels until she found a movie she remembered from her youth, watching it until she dozed off.

Around four in the morning, she was awakened by Julian as he crawled clumsily into bed.

"How was the party?" she asked sleepily.

"Great," he slurred. "Those guys are a blast. You shoulda seen the stuff they put together. There was a stripper, an' an open bar, an' somebody found these vintage porns with a girl who looked just like you!" He laughed drunkenly. "She was H-O-T hot, Evie. Evie! That was her name too."

Evelyn was wide awake now. "Really? That's odd."

"Not really. I mean, everyone has a doppelganger. Yours just happens to be a porn star from the turn of the century."

The chill that ran through her body was electric. Her life as Evie Ingenue came back in a rush of erotic imagery. She allowed Buck to guide her path as a porn star, and he made millions on her body. In truth, she had done well also. But her conservative Catholic upbringing had led her to feel guilty about enjoying her work as much as she did. The only thing that kept the guilt at bay was a steady supply of mood-altering chemicals which eventually ravaged her body and left her skinny and teetering on the edge of insanity.

She had trouble believing in God -- either the angry Catholic one or the loving Father of the non-denominational church Alan once led. If there were a god, would he allow man to cheat death? She doubted it.

Julian was already snoring beside her, but her mind wouldn't let her slip back into unconsciousness. Instead, she stepped out of bed and found her swimsuit. She padded down the stairs and through the great room to the patio doors. She plunged into the pool and swam laps in the chilled water, unable to think of anything besides her (hopefully buried) past. She wondered if Megan had found that part of her life too. If she had, she hadn't said anything to Evelyn about it. Keeping Marty's last name may have helped to hide Evie Ingenue, but she didn't know for sure. When she was married to Alan, her past was an open secret -- a point of pride for her pastor-husband. He often called her his Rahab, his scarlet woman with a heart of gold. Knowing what she already knew, Megan wouldn't have to scratch too deeply to discover the truth.

Of course, she consoled herself, Buck Naked was long dead, as were many of her co-stars. In general, porn stars weren't a long-lived bunch. If Alan hadn't come along and pulled her out of the life, she figured she would have been dead by thirty-five, if not sooner. Buck had lived into his fifties before keeling over one day from a heart attack. She had assumed his films had gone out of print after his death.

Curious, she finished her current lap and stepped out of the pool into the cool Las Vegas morning. Drying herself off, she walked back into the house and picked up her tablet computer, which was sitting on the large granite kitchen island. Opening her web browser, she searched for Evie Ingenue. To her horror, a list of fansites and vintage film retailers populated her screen. She clicked on the first fansite and read:

"Evelyn Mendoza, better known as Evie Ingenue, was born in the late 1980s. By all accounts she had a privileged childhood. Her parents were first-generation immigrants to the United States, but, unlike so many of their compatriots, they left Mexico to protect their wealth, not to escape poverty. They settled in a comfortable suburb of San Diego, California, and soon found employment in their fields. Evelyn and her two sisters all received private Catholic educations.

"The Great Housing Bubble burst just as Evelyn was finishing high school. The Mendozas, who were heavily invested in real estate, found themselves without funds for the first time in their lives. Their two older daughters were left with the responsibility of caring for the Mendozas and their youngest sister. Perhaps out of jealousy over young Evelyn's beauty, they refused to pay for her college education. Instead, they insisted that she find a job."

Evelyn laughed. This guy's take on her life was off by ten miles -- she was no mistreated waif. Her family had fallen on hard times, as had many others during the financial crisis. Shaking her head, she found the place where she had left off.

"Evelyn met Buck Naked while working as a waitress in an all-night cafe. Buck lured her in with the promise of fame and fortune. He renamed her Evie Ingenue and created a series of now-classic porn flicks around her, starting with *The 20-Year-Old Virgin* and ending abruptly six years later with *Life of Pie*. Evie Ingenue abandoned her career and vanished from the public stage.

"Where is Evie now? I attempted to track her down using what little I knew about her. It appears that she left the porn industry to marry a preacher. She had two children with him before eventually leaving the family. After that, her whereabouts become murky. She never held another job outside of the porn industry. I have tracked down marriage licenses for half a dozen Evelyn Mendozas, but none of them match our Evie's supposed birthdate. If she is still alive, she would be over sixty now. It's hard to picture the flexible girl known as Evie Ingenue as a senior citizen. Thinking about it too long will lead to mental images that will definitely curb your desire for her. However, thanks to Buck Naked, we will always have the young and beautiful version of Evie Ingenue."

Evelyn couldn't help the shiver that went down her spine. Even if someone did track her down, she reasoned, they would never believe that she was the same woman.

She climbed the steps to the master bedroom and tiptoed through it to the bathroom, closing the door behind her. Stripping off her bathing suit, she turned on the hot water tap in the bathtub. She turned to examine her body in the mirror over the sink. The signature tattoo she had once sported on the inside of her thigh was gone. The scars of childbirth were a distant memory. The life she once lived was no more than a story inside her brain. If the only way to keep it at bay was to pretend she didn't have family, she was prepared to do that.

She slid into the steaming water and let it soak away her doubts.

#

Evelyn was working a crummy diner job when Buck Naked spotted her. His name wasn't really Buck -- he had been born Seymour Jaffe in Detroit about thirty-five years before to a single mother who already had three other kids.

His father had been just another loser who passed through Jackie Jaffe's life, staying just long enough to plant his seed in her all-too-accommodating womb. Buck inherited three things from his absentee father: a silver tongue, an impressive package, and a lack of regard for anyone whose interests didn't coincide with his own. By the time he sat down in the diner where Evelyn waited tables, he had moved from on-screen talent to directing and producing his own skin flicks. He was only in town to scout for new talent, which happened to be in abundance at the strip club about two hundred feet away.

Of course, Evelyn didn't recognize him. Her father, the only man she had ever had the opportunity to get to know well, wasn't the porn-watching type. When he wasn't working, he was spending time with her mother and the rest of the family. Evie knew porn existed -- she wasn't that naive. But it simply wasn't part of her world. When she flashed her beautiful smile at Buck, she had no idea who she was looking at or what he would do to her world.

"Aren't you a beauty!" he said, giving her a low whistle.

She felt fire rise to her cheeks. "Thanks," she mumbled. "What can I get you?"

"I'll have a coffee and a few minutes of your time."

"I'll bring you the coffee, but I'm afraid I'm busy."

Buck glanced around the nearly empty shop. "Sweetheart, it's nearly two a.m. and I'm one of three customers in this joint. Take a break and give me a chance."

She thought he was attractive. Even in his dress shirt and tie, she could see his arms bulging beneath the fabric. He had baked-in crows' feet in the corners of his eyes. She imagined he might be a surfer or a bodybuilder -- both were fairly common in the state, if not in her hometown. He didn't look threatening. "Who are you?" she asked bluntly.

He smiled and said, "Name's Buck. What's yours?"

"Evelyn."

"Evelyn, will you have coffee with me?"

She nodded and walked to the coffee machine to get two cups. Before she went back to the table, she refilled the cup of the guy at the counter and took payment from the other table -- a couple who looked strung out on something other than caffeine.

When she returned to him, Buck was busily tapping away on his smartphone. She waited patiently for him to finish.

"How old are you?" he asked, pushing the phone to one side of the table.

"Eighteen."

"Good! Just right, in fact. And do you have a boyfriend?"

She shook her head. "I went to an all-girls' school. There weren't a lot of dating opportunities."

"Interesting. I knew you had a purity vibe about you. How does a girl from a private school end up working in an all-night diner?"

"I needed a job and this one was available."

"What if I told you that you could make what you make in a month here for just a few hours work?"

Evelyn's skin prickled. "Listen, I'm not interested in stripping--"

He laughed. "Strippers don't make the kind of money we're talking about. Strippers dream of climbing the ladder to the opportunity I'm offering you."

"I don't think I should be talking to you."

"What's the harm in listening?"

"I'm in college. I'll be a news reporter someday."

He smirked. "Okay, college girl...wouldn't you like a little more time to study? Working here and taking classes must be nearly impossible."

She cast her eyes down at the table, remembering the one community-college class she had already dropped. Even with the lighter load, she was struggling to keep up with the demands of four professors. If she dropped another class, she wouldn't qualify as a full-time student anymore. "I'm muddling through."

He reached across the table and took her fingers in his hand. Smiling kindly, he said, "Think of me as your fairy godfather. I'm here to save you from a life lived in greasy spoons and trailer parks."

She looked around the shabby restaurant and shuddered. "You really think I'll be stuck here?"

"Are you eating the food?" he asked. "Of course you are. Your metabolism can handle it now, but in another year or two, your body will start to pack on the pounds. Spending all your time inside, you'll lose your natural glow. By the time you're twenty-five, your dreams of being a newscaster will be a distant memory. You might have your degree, but no one at the networks is going to hire a greasy-spoon waitress who graduated from Podunk College when they could have a sophisticated woman from Harvard or another Ivy League school."

She swallowed back the tears.

"Let me guess: your brothers and sisters all got the good educations, right? Mom and Dad plopped down thousands of dollars to make sure they had bright futures, but when it was time for you to go...sorry! All out of cash."

"The housing bubble--"

"Was bound to burst. Anyone with sense could see that coming years ago. Your parents should have put your college money somewhere safe! They raised you to believe that your education was important, but then they let you work in a diner and compromise your future? They're just like everyone else in this world -- always looking out for themselves above all."

"No, they're good parents...they didn't know the stock market was going to crash too. They wanted me to go to a better college, but--"

He shrugged. "Okay. Believe what you must. I'm just some guy in a diner." He pointed out the window at the black vintage muscle car parked right outside. "But that's my ride." He flashed his gold watch at her. "This is my everyday timepiece." He opened his wallet and pulled out a black American Express card. "And that's how I'm paying for my coffee."

She slumped back against the booth, defeated. "What are you doing in a diner at this time of the night?"

He pointed his chin in the direction of the strip club. "Scouting."

"Didn't you find anything over there?"

"A couple of girls who would be good second stringers. I'm looking for star quality -- and you've got it."

"Why do you think that?"

"First of all, you're beautiful. I'm guessing you're a virgin, and virgins play well for a certain audience. And some men like to follow a girl from her first sexual experience on. It's a very particular audience, but I see a whole series: The Education of Evelyn."

"I couldn't use my real name," she said before slapping a hand over her mouth.

"It's all right," he soothed. "I know this is the first time you've ever thought of anything like this. But this is your chance to veer away from the path you've started down. I know you want a more exciting life. Let me help you."

"I need to think about it."

"Fine. I understand. I'll be in town another couple days. Do you work Friday night?"

She nodded.

"I'll stop by then and we'll see where we are." He opened his wallet again and handed her a business card.

Buck Naked, Director/Producer, Buck Naked Films. She blushed again.

Chapter 10 Marty

"Evelyn, this is my partner Marty. Marty, this is my sister Evelyn." Carmen frowned slightly.

Evelyn didn't know what she was so worried about -- short, round, balding doctors weren't exactly her type.

"A pleasure," he said, taking her hand and brushing his lips against it lightly.

Evelyn giggled. "Mine as well. I've heard a lot about you."

"You can't trust a thing this one says," he answered with a conspiratorial wink.

"She said you were funny."

"A lie straight from Hades."

"We should go," Carmen interjected. "Marty still has patients to see."

"Just one. Why don't you wait? I'd love to take you both to dinner."

"We really can't. We have--"

"Nothing so very important," Evelyn interrupted. Carmen shot her a look full of daggers. Evelyn smiled sweetly.

"Wonderful! Just give me ten minutes. I've got to tell my favorite hypochondriac that she's still not dying." He walked back through the door that led from the waiting room to the exam rooms of his and Carmen's practice.

"Why did you do that?" Carmen whined.

"Because you seemed so against it."

"Listen: Marty is a nice guy. I know what you do to nice guys. Look at poor Alan."

"Alan and I were married for almost twenty years."

"And then you ripped out his heart and stomped on it right in front of him."

"It wasn't like that."

"You could have fooled me."

Evelyn looked away from her sister, choosing instead to examine the art on the walls of the office. "Where do they sell this crap?" she said as she reached out a hand to touch the piece made of various shades of wood. It reminded her of a display in a flooring store.

"Don't touch that!" Carmen snapped. "We paid a small fortune for it."

"Why? I could have made it for you with a few planks of wood from Home Depot."

"You just don't understand modern art, Evie. This is a very soothing piece."

"It might be soothing, but it's not very interesting." She moved on to the landscape featuring two palm trees. "Let me guess: it's all about relaxation?"

"We are a medical practice, Evelyn."

Evelyn smiled to herself before she turned to face Carmen again. "What does that have to do with anything?"

"Studies show that abstract art and realistic landscapes are calming to people. Since patients generally come to us when they are in distress, the artwork is meant to give them a sense of peace."

"And I suppose surrealism doesn't do that?"

"No," she answered sourly, "not at all."

A woman slightly older than her sister emerged from the back of the office with an expression of relief. "Thank you, Dr. Bryant!" she called over her shoulder. She smiled at Carmen and Evelyn before leaving the office.

Marty emerged, rubbing his hands together vigorously. Evelyn assumed he had just applied some anti-bacterial cleaner to them. "Well? Shall we?"

"Don't you want to change first?" Evelyn asked.

He raised his eyebrows. "Suit yourself, but the white coat tends to get us seated in a hurry!"

"Seriously?"

He laughed as he shrugged the coat off. "Nah. I haven't actually worn it to a restaurant since I was an intern. Back then I wanted to wear it everywhere I went. But then I dumped spaghetti sauce down the front of one and didn't have a backup readily available...I kinda changed my mind after that."

Evelyn laughed and Marty seemed to stand up a little straighter.

Carmen led the way out of the office. Marty gallantly stepped aside and swept his arm wide, indicating that Evelyn should leave the room ahead of him. He followed her out and locked the door behind them. As he did so, he said quietly, "Carmen never mentioned how beautiful you were."

"That's sweet of you to say."

He glanced at her and said, "I'm not just blowing smoke. You are a beautiful woman."

"Thank you." She had to admit he had great eyes -- warm, deep, and dark umber. She let him take her arm as they walked toward the elevator. Evelyn saw Carmen's warning expression and chose to ignore it. "How is it that a man such as yourself is unattached?"

"I'm married to my practice, I suppose. My first three wives didn't like being in second position to the office."

"You spend a lot of time working?"

"He's there before I come in and after I leave," Carmen answered.

"Yes, but lately I've been thinking about shortening my hours...maybe even doing some traveling." He smiled at the two women.

134

"Seriously? You think you could last a week outside of this place?"

"I'm willing to give it a try...if the right companion comes along." He clicked his car's remote and Evelyn saw the lights flash on a hunter-green Jaguar. "Why don't you ride with me? I can drive you back here after dinner."

"I don't like to leave my car in the parking lot after hours. We'll meet you there."

"Don't make me drive alone, Carmen. At least let me have your sister to talk to."

Carmen pursed her lips.

Evelyn knew that her sister had been planning to accost her about flirting with Marty; she was glad for the escape route. "Of course I'll ride with you, Marty," she said, batting her eyelashes a few times.

"Fine. I'll meet the two of you there." Carmen stormed off in the direction of her sedan as Marty opened the passenger door of his car for her. She slid in and inhaled the musky scent of his cologne, which had permeated the car through years of habitual use. The soft leather seat enveloped her; she felt as if she could easily fall asleep in the vehicle.

Marty slid into the other side of the car and pressed the start button. "So," he asked, "where were we?"

"Three marriages?"

"I'm afraid so. I'm either a bad judge of character or a terrible husband. But you must have been married before, as well. Didn't Carmen tell me that you were recently divorced?"

"It's been about a year now."

"May I ask what happened?"

"I tried to be someone I wasn't until I simply couldn't pretend anymore," she sighed.

"I can't imagine why you would need to be anyone other than who you are."

"You barely know me. You may disagree after a few weeks."

Marty was silent, as if he were absorbing her words. They were driving along the winding road that led to the small restaurant where they had agreed to meet Carmen. "I don't want to be who I've been for the last twenty years. I'm tired, Evelyn. I'm ready to do something else."

"What do you want to do?"

"I've always wanted to travel. When I was younger -- right after I finished my internship, in fact -- I almost signed up for this medical charity that sends doctors into third-world countries."

"Why didn't you?"

"I proposed to my first wife and she said yes. If she had turned me down, my life would be completely different. Maybe I'd be working in Africa or South America right now." He turned into the parking lot of their destination. "What about you? Where would you be if you hadn't married your ex?"

"Dead," she answered.

He laughed uncomfortably. "You don't have much faith in yourself."

"No. But I had a lot of faith in him."

Carmen was already standing in front of the restaurant. Marty turned off the car and they both exited the Jaguar.

"How did you get so far behind me?" Carmen asked. "You pulled out of the lot ahead of me."

"Haven't we had this conversation before? You're actually supposed to obey the speed-limit signs, not just read them." He nudged her shoulder good-naturedly. "Thanks for loaning me Evelyn."

"The hostess said she could seat us as soon as you arrived. They're not too busy tonight."

"Good. I don't know about you ladies, but I'm starving."

"You wouldn't be if you would stop and eat lunch."

He shrugged. "My patients are used to a certain level of service."

"You mean they're like spoiled children." Carmen turned to Evelyn. "He leaves two appointments open for

136

emergency visits, but tells our receptionist to never turn away any of his patients who need immediate appointments. Sometimes he sees twenty patients in a day -- especially during flu season."

"You just admire my dedication."

The trio walked to the hostess station and followed a tall young woman to their table. "Your server will be with you momentarily," she said as she handed each of them menus.

As soon as she walked away, Carmen asked, "So, what did you two talk about on your way here?"

"You," Marty answered. "Nothing but you. What a great sister you are, what an amazing partner..."

Carmen rolled her eyes. "Fine. Don't tell me."

"We just got to know each other, that's all. Your ears shouldn't have been burning."

The waiter appeared and took their drink orders. The three of them fell into silence as they perused the menus.

"What do you recommend?" Evelyn finally asked Marty. "This was your choice, right?"

"Yeah," he answered. "I come here pretty regularly. Let's see...do you like pasta?"

"Yes."

"Then I suggest the penne with chicken sausage. They use this pink vodka sauce on it that is different from anything I've ever had before. I've never seen it anywhere else around here, either."

"Sounds delicious." Evelyn closed her menu and smiled at Marty, who smiled back.

"I think I just talked myself into having the same thing." He reached out and Evelyn handed him her menu. He stacked his and hers together in the empty fourth spot on the table. "What about you, Carmen?"

"I'm still looking," she answered.

The waiter returned with the drinks. "Is everyone ready to order?"

"Go ahead," Carmen said. "I'll be ready in a second."

"Madam?" he asked, looking at Evelyn.

"She and I will have the penne and chicken sausage," Marty answered for her.

"Would either of you like a salad to start?"

"Not for me. Just bring more bread."

"Yes, please," Evelyn said. "Balsamic vinaigrette."

"Are you ready to order?" the waiter asked, looking directly at Carmen.

She sighed and frowned. "I suppose I'll just have the eggplant Parmesan."

"Is there something you would like that isn't on the menu? It's a slow night... I'm sure the kitchen would be happy to accommodate you."

"What I really would like is a simple breast of chicken prepared with olive oil, salt, and pepper."

"That's not a problem," he answered.

"Could I get a small side of noodles with butter and Parmesan too?"

"Of course. I'll be back with more bread in a few minutes."

"Not in the mood for Italian?" Marty questioned.

"I guess not. Nothing sounded good. And my stomach is a bit touchy."

Evelyn figured that Carmen's stomach complaint had more to do with Evelyn meeting Marty than anything else.

"You don't have to stay if you don't want to. I'd be happy to drive Evelyn home after dinner."

"No, no...I've ordered now. Besides, you're practically home."

Marty shrugged and changed the subject, and soon their conversation was flowing. If Carmen was a little quieter than usual, Marty didn't seem to notice. When the meals arrived, the conversation slowed but didn't stop. Evelyn agreed that the pasta dish Marty suggested was excellent. Carmen's dinner looked considerably less exciting, though she said it was perfect.

By the time Evelyn and her sister parted company with the plump and amiable doctor, Evelyn knew exactly why Carmen didn't want her to meet him: Carmen was in love with her partner.

"Why don't you tell him you're interested?" Evelyn prodded her sister over breakfast the next morning.

"Because it's one of our rules: keep romance out of the office." Carmen was preparing a cup of coffee for herself; she didn't bother to meet her sister's eyes.

"But you're never not going to work together! In fact, you're probably both each other's main reason for continuing to work."

She laughed bitterly. "He's been my business partner through three marriages now. I don't think he only had eyes for me."

Evelyn waved her sister's objection away. "Some people can't be alone. Marty needs a girlfriend or a wife. You aren't available, so he makes other arrangements."

She turned around and leaned against the cabinet. "All three of his wives have accused me of being the other woman," she mused.

"Just because you aren't sleeping together doesn't mean you aren't having an affair."

"Don't be ridiculous." She pushed off the counter and walked briskly toward her room. Over her shoulder, she called, "Stay out of this, Evelyn. It's none of your business."

Evelyn knew that Carmen meant it. But she also knew that her sister was lonely -- she always had been.

Carmen was the least attractive of the Mendoza sisters. Evelyn's mother once told her that Carmen got a little too much DNA from their distant Native American ancestors. Carmen's skin color earned her the more-ethnic name as well. Evelyn and Karen, who were both born fair-skinned, received names that were intended to blend well with their private-school counterparts.

Not that Carmen didn't go to the same schools -- she did. Their parents were pragmatic people who, unlike most Mexican parents, believed that their daughters should receive the best education possible. Her father didn't care about having a son to carry on the family name; her mother wanted her daughters to be successful without needing to rely on men. They encouraged Carmen to follow her passion for science and they were rewarded with a brilliant medical student. When Karen wanted to pursue an MBA, they supported her choice; she found work on Wall Street right after graduation.

Evelyn was the youngest by nearly seven years. Her sisters were already out living their own lives by the mid-2000s. Evelyn enjoyed a quiet and comfortable adolescence with her parents. She didn't rebel; she studied hard. She was smart and, according to her mother, more beautiful than any of the women in their family had been in generations. Evelyn remembered the picture her mother kept on the wall of her bedroom of her long-dead ancestor. The woman in it was beautiful -- pale with dark hair and eyes that were slightly upturned at the outer corners. She was dressed beautifully, as befitted a woman of her status at the time. Dona Maria Carmelita Santiago. Through this woman, her mother's family traced their roots back to Spain. When Evelyn told her mother that she wanted to be like Barbara Walters, her mother grinned and said, "You will be bigger than her, for you are so much more beautiful."

But then the housing bubble burst and the stock market fell and her parents were both laid off. Karen was fired and moved back home. Evelyn's college fund dried up. Carmen became the sole support of the family. Her oldest sister seemed angry for years, and Evelyn understood why: her best years -- her best chance to find love -- were instead swallowed up by her family obligations.

Marty called Evelyn a few days after that first dinner. "I had a wonderful time with you and your sister."

"I did too. Now I know why Carmen is so fond of you."

"We've been friends and colleagues for decades now...I can't imagine my life without her."

"Here's hoping you never have to."

"Listen...the reason I'm calling...I have tickets to a play tonight and I was wondering if you'd like to go with me."

"Maybe you should ask Carmen. She would probably love a night out."

"Carmen's not really the Shakespeare type."

Evelyn couldn't refute his argument: Carmen had always said she thought the playwright was overrated. Hesitantly, she asked, "Why do you have two tickets for the play in the first place?"

"Habit. My last wife and I had a season subscription for the Shakespearean troupe. I renewed it without reviewing the bill carefully."

"For how many years?"

He chuckled. "You got me. I like to have tickets handy as a way of getting beautiful women to spend time with me."

She laughed. "I guess you couldn't find a beauty this time, huh?"

"On the contrary," he said soberly, "I've found someone who is not only gorgeous, but also interesting."

She couldn't laugh off his words again without hurting his feelings. "Okay. I'll go with you. What are we seeing?"

"*Taming of the Shrew*."

#

Their courtship was brief. After just three months, Marty proposed to Evelyn during a short weekend trip to Crater Lake. Even as she had tried to talk up her sister, Evelyn had fallen in love with Marty. She said yes immediately.

"How could you do this to me?" Carmen asked when Evelyn, wearing a gaudy diamond ring, announced the news.

"You said you didn't want him."

"That didn't mean you could have him!" Carmen, in a rare show of irritation, threw her crystal wineglass across the room, leaving a spray of red liquid on the wall and shards of glass on the floor.

"I'm sorry, Carmen. I didn't mean for this to happen."

"You broke our parents' hearts when you stumbled into porn. You fell into Alan's arms and ruined his life. You abandoned your children when you accidentally destroyed your marriage. You've never done a damn thing right! And yet." Her hands were clenched; Evelyn could see her fingernails digging into the meat of her palms. "You don't deserve him! He is a good man, Evelyn, and all you ever do is destroy good people!"

Evelyn left her sister screaming in the kitchen and hastily packed a bag. When she slipped out the front door, she could hear her sister's mournful wails from outside the house. She walked to the curb and dialed Marty's phone.

"Hello, sweetheart."

"Hi, Marty. Could I stay at your house tonight? Carmen...isn't feeling well and wants to be alone."

"Of course."

#

Marty talked to Carmen the next day in the office. Evelyn never knew exactly what Marty said, but her sister called and apologized. Their relationship was never quite the same until after Marty was gone though.

Marty gave Evelyn free reign to plan any sort of wedding she wanted. They went to Las Vegas to see a few venues, but ultimately she chose a different destination -- the U.S. Virgin Islands. She asked her kids to come, but only Desmond, who was seventeen by then, agreed. Hope chose to stay with her father. Marty's daughters, all three of them in their late teens or early twenties, came as well. Carmen said she wished she could come, but someone had to stay and run the practice, especially with Marty retiring.

So, one beautiful day in the Caribbean, Marty and Evelyn were married as four of their children looked on. Marty's daughters never really warmed to Evelyn, but then they barely knew the woman, before or after the wedding. As it turned out, all three of the girls were much more familiar with Desmond.

The original plan had been to spend two weeks in paradise and return to Oregon. After just seven days though, Marty decided that they weren't going home -- maybe not ever. Of course, Evelyn agreed wholeheartedly. From their island honeymoon, they traveled to England and then to the European mainland, gradually working their way south to Portugal before hopping to the African continent for a six-month safari.

Marty missed the births of three grandchildren. Evelyn missed first Desmond's and then Hope's high school graduations. None of that mattered, because Marty and Evelyn only had eyes for each other.

As they were meandering their way back up the coast of the continent, they intersected with an ocean-going medical charity. Marty, who had once dreamed of working on just such a boat, jumped at the chance to join the staff; Evelyn happily settled into the small suite to which they were assigned. If anyone recognized her from her porn-star past, no one said a word about it. She was accepted by the other spouses, and even found she enjoyed volunteering on clinic days. She comforted children in terrible pain and held the hands of women hideously deformed by growths and tumors. She learned thankfulness in a way she never had as the wife of a preacher.

Each night, when she and Marty fell into bed in their tiny cabin, they held hands and talked about what they had seen. Their marriage and their travels had brought them both to a place of contentment that they assumed would last the rest of their lives.

They were on the ship for nearly ten years in the end. When one was ready to leave, the other would want to stay. Each of them knew the right words to convince the one with wanderlust to stay a little longer. When they finally packed their bags and left the charity, their fellow citizens -- for the boat was like a floating city -- threw them a going-away party. Marty and Evelyn nearly changed their minds at the party, but their friends insisted it was time for them to move on. After all, they had spent their honeymoon years taking care of the people of Africa.

The next morning, they stepped off the boat and kept walking for the first time in a decade. Cape Town, South Africa, was a beautiful city, and the people were friendly. They found a cafe and settled in for a good breakfast while they considered their options.

"I can't believe we actually left," Marty said as he sipped his coffee.

"We've been talking about it for so long, it had started to feel like a fantasy," Evelyn laughed. "So, what do we do now? Head back to Oregon?"

Marty looked out the window, watching the well-dressed locals stride purposefully down the sidewalks. "We've seen so many hurting people for so many years, it's hard to believe this city is even on the same continent."

She nodded. "I know what you mean."

"I spent so much of my life -- before you, of course -- helping people with their first-world problems. Somewhere, in the back of my mind, I knew people were actually suffering...but I never saw them in my office." He pointed to a young woman in a blue pantsuit moving briskly past the cafe. "Do you suppose she knows that only a few hundred miles from here people are suffering?"

Evelyn smiled at her husband. "You want to go back to the boat."

He took her hand. "No. But what about the people who can't travel to the docks? The people who live so far inland that the Mercy ships might as well be stars in the sky?"

Evelyn's eyes widened as she understood Marty's meaning. "You want to move inland? To set up a clinic? Where?"

"I don't know yet. Niger? Chad? The Congo? Somewhere we can make a difference."

"I know you have a lot of money from the sale of your practice and the house, but do you really think we have enough to open a clinic? And what if the money runs out? It's not like the patients we would be serving would be able to pay us."

"You think I'm being ridiculous."

"No! Not at all. But I do think we need to consider the practicalities."

He withdrew his hand. "It's not fair of me to put you in an even more uncomfortable living situation than we've been in for the last decade."

She sat back in her chair and gazed out the window at the cosmopolitan city. They hadn't been in a city like this one since the early days of their marriage, but she didn't miss the modern conveniences or the culture as much as she thought she had. In fact, the walk to the cafe had been overwhelming -

- like sensory overload. She shifted her gaze to Marty. "Whither thou goest, I will go."

"Isn't that from the Book of Ruth? She was following her mother-in-law, you know."

Evelyn grinned. "The thought behind it is what matters."

#

Evelyn and Marty only went back stateside to raise money for the clinic they planned to open. Carmen, who knew they had nowhere to stay, invited them to use her guest room. Ten years of absence had changed Carmen's heart toward Evelyn -- she welcomed her sister back with all the joy of one finding a long-lost relative. She embraced Marty as her brother.

Marty and Evelyn met their grandchildren for the first time -- though Evelyn was unaware that three of them were, in fact, her grandchildren. Two of Marty's daughters had met and married good men. The third was raising a daughter, whom Evelyn found remarkably like her daughter Hope, on her own. None of the children seemed all that interested in meeting their grandparents; Marty was disappointed, but Evelyn told him that their disregard was normal for children who had never met them before.

Evelyn flew to Phoenix to meet Hope and her family. She wasn't surprised to find her granddaughter was well-behaved and polite. Little Abigail sat quietly at her mother's side as Evelyn and Hope attempted polite conversation.

"I understand you married a doctor," Glen, Hope's husband, said.

"Yes. Marty and I have been working on a Mercy ship for the last several years."

"Really?" asked Hope. "That must have been his idea, right?"

"Well...yes. But I found the lifestyle to be very rewarding."

"You know father wanted us to be a missionary family. He said you refused."

"He never asked me. He just assumed I wouldn't want to do it."

Her daughter raised one eyebrow and stared at her doubtfully.

"I might have made noises like I wouldn't," she conceded, "but I would have followed him wherever he wanted to go."

The silence that followed was so uncomfortable that Glen squirmed in his seat. Finally, when it became clear that neither mother nor daughter intended to give in, he cleared his throat and said, "So, what's Africa like?"

Evelyn, relieved, answered, "It's like nothing you've ever seen here. It's wild and untamed in most places, yet urban in others. The people are resilient and yet superstitious." She told them about the children she had comforted and the miracles she had seen the doctors perform.

"You abandoned us to take care of thousands of others," Hope interpreted when Evelyn stopped talking. "I don't understand how any mother could do such a thing."

Chapter 11 Evelyn and Julian

The most shocking part of the Cure -- even more shocking than the physical regeneration of the elderly -- was what it did to children. When administered to them, they grew. Within a month of receiving Promorterem, the children reached full physical maturity. Imagine the problem of having full-grown adult bodies -- including all the sexual urges -- inhabited by the minds of infants. The researchers deemed this to be Promoterem's only true failure. But the failure was so spectacular that it came to represent the most devastating fear of the drug. For most of the Fifties, the drug was a political hot potato that the major parties tossed back and forth. Each accused the other of secretly supporting -- and even funding -- the drug as a way of maintaining political offices indefinitely at the expense of the very people they claimed to represent. They paraded the "victims" across the media stage -- these poor children who would never have childhoods. What they left out of their speeches was the small detail that their "victims" were pulled from the foster care system. The state already served as parents to them -- and the state was almost worse than the abusive homes these children were removed from. Indifferent to the fate of their wards, those charged with their care allowed them to be used as political pawns.

Despite the political power plays, the parents whose children were actually saved by the drug praised it. It didn't

148

matter that their children were now walking around in adult bodies; what matter was that they were walking around at all. The chorus of grateful families was barely a hum at the beginning of the decade. By the end of it, their songs of joy were drowning out the politicians who hadn't already switched sides.

In January 2063, the final nail was pounded into the coffin of the opposition...literally. The most vocal opponent, a senator from Kentucky whom everyone knew as Ol' Red, died. The day of his funeral, the Supreme Court opted not to review the final case brought against Mose Baxter to prevent the widespread distribution of the drug. By February, every female movie star in America looked as young and fresh as when they were ingenues. Of course, some of the male movie stars did too, but not as many -- gray hair and fine lines on men were still desirable.

With cameras rolling, Evelyn married Julian. The wedding preempted a Saturday-morning cooking show and the local Humane Society's weekly pet parade. None of Evelyn's family attended; her side of the chapel was filled with fans of the local news team instead.

Evelyn wore the dress Megan picked out for her, carried the flowers Megan said looked best on television, and strolled down a red aisle because, according to Megan, that was the only color that made sense.

When she kissed Julian at the end of the ceremony, she sent up a silent prayer that Marty would forgive her.

She and Julian shared a brief honeymoon in the sky-high suite Megan secured for them, which was housed at the top of one of the four spires and featured 360-degree views of the Nevada city and its surrounding desert. The honeymoon itself was over before the end of the three-day weekend. This was, after all, more of a business arrangement than an actual marriage.

The couple returned to work on the Tuesday following their nuptials.

#

"Good news!" Megan announced as she swept into the studio. Nearly six years had passed since the resplendent wedding. "Philadelphia likes what they see on the tapes. They want to fly you two in for an interview. If it goes well, the three of us will have one hell of a gig!"

Julian wrinkled his nose. "Isn't it cold there? I was really hoping for L.A."

"Los Angeles isn't interested at this time. Maybe in a few years. They think you look too young to be taken seriously."

"That's a joke. That town runs on youth," Evelyn said.

"Only in the entertainment district. Apparently, they like their news to feel more solid." Megan flexed playfully. "But never mind them. Philadelphia is a huge market and they're close to New York! Which, of course, is where we all want to be, right?"

Evelyn nodded, but Julian just pouted.

Megan rolled her eyes. "Come on now. You'll be leaving Las Vegas on top of the heap -- that's the best time to leave, believe me!" When Julian didn't seem inclined to agree, Megan said, "Evie, talk to him. It's in both your best interests." She turned on her heel and left the studio.

"What's wrong, Julian?"

"I want L.A.! I don't want to have to slog my way through snow ever again. Why is that so hard to understand?"

"But if L.A. isn't an option right now..."

"Then we should just stay here. Vegas is good enough."

The news director cleared her throat; Evelyn glanced at her and smiled. "We'll talk about this later," she said, heading toward the news desk.

"Nothing to talk about," Julian grumbled.

"In five, four, three," the director said.

"Good evening, Las Vegas!" Julian said brightly. "In tonight's news, the latest controversy surrounding the miracle cure, Promorterem..."

Evelyn's smile only faltered for a second.

# # #

On their days off from reading the news, the couple preferred to stay home. Evelyn rediscovered her love of cooking -- a hobby she had picked up during her marriage to Alan. She wowed Julian with dishes not normally found on restaurant menus, like Beef Wellington and creamed corn.

For his part, Julian became an avid reader. He borrowed from Evelyn's digital collection, which she had built up over the decades. He had marveled at the more than two-thousand books she had stored. "You've read all of these?"

"No. A few...maybe a couple hundred at best."

"Why do you have so many?" he laughed. "I don't think I've seen you read anything but news articles."

"Before I went to work at the station, I read a lot. Remember, you were gone most of the time."

He accepted that answer and dove into her collection with enthusiasm.

Though their marriage was nothing like the one she shared with Marty, Evelyn appreciated the companionship Julian provided. They were each other's closest friend and perfect roommates. The passion she had once felt for him was long gone, but she was comfortable with the thought of spending the rest of her life with him.

By the time Megan approached them with the Philadelphia job offer, Evelyn had convinced him to get a vasectomy. She knew that she didn't want any more children, and she wanted to be certain that no one would pop up claiming to be the mother of Julian's offspring. Their marriage was a major factor in their value as a commodity -- nothing would be allowed to destroy that.

Their made-for-television romance was little more than a show. If it weren't for the hectic schedule their jobs forced them to keep, Evie had no doubt that Julian would be on the prowl for sexual partners. As it was, she was fairly certain he was receiving special, personal attention from the makeup artist and the craft-services girl. But as long as it didn't detract from the illusion, Evie was more than willing to accept his wandering eye.

The only thing that could pry the two of them out of their McMansion was the charity Megan had assigned to them: a cancer foundation for children. After her years on the Mercy ship, Evelyn had a natural affection for medical charities and was good with sick children. Julian, who was somewhat put off by illness, had a harder time with the visits and appearances. However, because his career was important to him and Megan said showing benevolence could be the key to bigger markets, Evelyn's vain partner managed to grin and bear the inconvenience of being empathetic.

The weekend after the Philadelphia job offer, Evelyn and Julian were scheduled to co-host a charity dinner at the Taj Mahal Casino. After several years as lead news anchor, she had a dozen evening gowns, which were purchased specifically for events like the one they were going to that night. Nevertheless, she pulled out the yellow dropped-waist dress she had purchased at the mall the day Ronnie first accused her of being an old woman masquerading as a youthful one. She slipped it over her head and walked back into the bedroom, where Julian was struggling with his cummerbund.

"Whoa," he said when he saw her. "I don't think I've seen that dress before."

She shrugged. "It's been in my closet since before we were married. Don't you like it?"

"Actually, it's very becoming on you. It reminds me of those old movies."

"You mean from the 1920s?"

"I was thinking of *The Great Gatsby*," he said with a laugh. "I don't think I've ever sat through anything that was produced before the turn of the century. Have you?"

"I've seen the stills," she lied, "in textbooks."

"That's right...you took that class on 20th-Century Media. I never understood why you bothered."

"It counted as a history credit." She spun in the dress. "Are you sure I look all right?"

"You're beautiful, as always. Come help me with this tie."

She stood in front of him and tied his bow tie with relative ease. Since Julian seemed unable to learn to tie it himself, Evelyn had spent a few hours practicing her technique. When she was done, she moved to one side and gazed at their reflections in the mirror. "We look like a fairytale couple."

"And so we are, aren't we?" He flashed his "sincere" smile -- the one he practiced when he thought she wasn't looking.

She thought they were the perfect Las Vegas couple: beautiful veneers that hid the mundane and the ugly. She glanced at the clock. "We should go, or we'll be late."

As he always did when they had to make an entrance at a Las Vegas event, Julian had hired a car to drive them. It was already awaiting them in the circle drive that fronted their home. The chauffeur, a beautiful girl in a black tie, opened the door for Evelyn as she approached the vehicle. She couldn't help but wonder if Julian would find an excuse to disappear from the event for fifteen minutes so that he could get to know this girl on a more intimate level. She shoved the thought to the back of her mind and tried to calm her mind. Live events with audiences were always so much more stressful than sitting behind the desk in the studio. Julian had the gift of gab and the ability to seem at ease in social situations like this one. For Evelyn, public appearances heightened her fear of being recognized as Evie Ingenue, even though that part of her life was nearly fifty years in the past.

Julian slid in on the other side of the car and put his hand over hers. "Geez, babe...your hands are like ice. Relax."

"I know. I just get anxious."

"I don't know why...you're always the most beautiful girl in the room."

She smiled at his well-meaning compliment. "Thank you, Jules."

"You'll be fine. You always are."

The car rolled out of the driveway and toward the city.

"Do you mind if I listen to some tunes?" Julian asked.

"Use the headphones, please. I would prefer silence."

He shrugged and pulled out a set of earbuds, plugging them into the car's audio system. He selected his choice of music -- a local band that was starting to get some national recognition -- on the touch screen of the center console.

She watched out the window as the car slid noiselessly through the streets. The recent city-wide ban on gas-powered vehicles had effectively eliminated noise pollution from even a city as loud as Vegas. Without having to contend with traffic sounds, the casinos didn't insist on pumping their music into the streets at levels proven to damage hearing anymore. The whole city felt friendlier to Evelyn. The people on the streets seemed happier.

The car turned into the Taj Mahal's drive and slid around to the front entrance -- a white-marble archway flanked by four turban-wearing men in embroidered tunics. As they left their car and approached the arch, a man on each side of it opened a door for Evelyn and Julian. As soon as they stepped in, Evelyn noticed the head swivels of about a quarter of the people in the lobby area -- average for a tourist spot in Vegas. Julian took her hand and led the way to the banquet room where the dinner was being held.

In the hallway outside the room, Megan was waiting for them. "Where have you been? You're supposed to be at the microphone in less than two minutes!"

"We're here, aren't we?" Julian answered irritably. "Why should we be early?"

Megan pursed her lips as she took Evelyn's clutch. She opened the door and said, "Go!"

The room's occupants burst into applause as soon as they were spotted. Julian turned on his smile and strode across the stage toward the microphone. "Good evening, ladies and gentlemen! Thank you so much for supporting this amazingly good cause." He swiveled and handed the mic to Evelyn, who smiled and batted her eyelashes.

"The Saving the Future Foundation is doing miraculous things today. In addition to providing fuel and food to the Mercy Ships that are helping people around the world right now, they are also providing scholarships to promising young people pursuing degrees in the medical field. Without these scholarships, many of these soon-to-be doctors and nurses would not be able to attend college at all." She paused to allow the audience to applaud, which, of course, they did. "Tonight, Saving the Future is pleased to introduce their newest board member. As a tech guru, he invented many of the applications we regularly use today. Instead of taking his billions of dollars and buying a tropical island paradise, he has reinvested his good luck in the human race. He is the primary source of funds supporting the continued research and development of Promorterem, which may very well save us all one day. Ladies and gentlemen, please welcome Mose Baxter!"

The applause was, at best, lukewarm. Evelyn and Julian shook the slightly plump, diminutive man's hand and left the stage. Baxter cleared his throat nervously and took a deep breath. "Well. I have to say first off that I've never been much of a public speaker. When the director of Saving the Future asked me to speak at this dinner, I initially said no." He blew out a shuddering breath and inhaled sharply. "But I wanted to address some of the concerns floating around about Promorterem, and this seemed like a good venue for that." He looked toward Evelyn, who was standing just behind the curtain to one side of him. "Miss, would you bring me a bottle of water?"

Evelyn looked behind her and spotted an open door that led to a hallway away from the stage. She headed toward it, hoping to spot a resort employee. Luckily, a young woman in a uniform met her at the door with a bottle of water. Thanking the girl, Evelyn loosened the cap as she walked back toward the stage. She could hear Baxter describing the process by which Promorterem worked using terminology only a double major in Computer Science and Molecular Biology could possibly understand. One look at the audience told her that he had already lost them. Baxter, however, seemed unaware of the glazed expressions before him. She cleared her throat.

"Ah! Thank you, my dear...just what I needed." He reached out for the bottle.

She took the opportunity to get close enough to whisper, "Stop telling them how it works; show them what it does!" When she pulled back, she could see the puzzled expression in his eyes. Fearing that he hadn't understood, she turned and walked off the stage.

He opened the bottle and took a long, slow pull on the contents. When he was done, he replaced the bottle cap and said, "Promorterem itself isn't that interesting, I suppose, unless you happen to be something of a science nerd. In essence, Promorterem is a nanobot that can fix anything that ails you. Let me show you exactly what that means."

He took a small device out of his pocket and clicked a button. Above him hovered an image of a severely disfigured person. "I'd like to introduce you to Maharene. Maharene has

Polyostotic Fibrous Dysplasia. If Maharene lived in a first-world country, her condition would have been treated immediately and monitored on a regular basis. Her face would never have been allowed to become so disfigured. However, because she lived in a rural, third-world African village that relies heavily on Mercy Ships for medical care, her life has been filled with fear, sadness, and pain. She watched others with her condition starve to death because they are unable to swallow around the growths that disfigure them. Her own mother threw her out of the family home when she was just thirteen because she believed Maharene was the source of the family's bad luck. Since the age of ten, Maharene has trekked to the Mercy ship every eighteen months for life-saving surgeries. Between visits, she woke each morning and examined her face for signs that the tumors were returning -- because they always do." Baxter ran through a series of photos, each one taken at a Mercy ship consultation.

Evelyn recognized the girl. She had only been ten years old the first time she had seen her. Marty treated her four times over the years, and each time, Evelyn held the girl's hand.

"Six months ago, on her last visit to the Mercy ship, Maharene was one of five hundred recipients of Promorterem. You see, since the Mercy ships are not in American waters, they can administer drugs that are not FDA approved."

A few gasps came from the audience, but only from the most innocent among them. Anyone with the kind of money that made this charity dinner a cheap date was too jaded to recognize the FDA as an authority in such matters.

The final picture appeared on the screen. A twentyish woman with close-cropped hair and big brown eyes filled the screen. Her high cheekbones and full lips gave her a radiant, healthy appearance. "This is Maharene today."

Unlike the previous gasps of outrage, the noise that came from the audience was filled with amazement.

"Just one dose of Promorterem was all it took to rewrite her body at a cellular level. At this time, all remnants of her previous disfiguring disease have been erased. Her DNA has been restored to what it was the day she was born. And she is healthy."

Evelyn felt a tear of joy rolled down her cheek. She carefully blotted it away with the back of her hand. As she lowered her arm, she felt it brush against someone standing just to the side of her. She turned to look and found Maharene standing there. She smiled at the young woman.

Maharene smiled back before confusion clouded her eyes. "Missus B?"

"...welcome Maharene to the stage!" Baxter said at the same moment.

Evelyn raised a hand and put it against the woman's shoulder, forcing her to move forward and into the spotlight.

Maharene blinked twice in the light and brought a hand up to shade her eyes.

Evelyn watched her from behind the curtains. The dress she wore was obviously made for her -- it fit better than anything she had ever seen the girl in before. It was the American version of tribal dress: the multicolored cloth covered her body from shoulder to toe. Someone had hung huge hoop earrings from her ears. Evelyn wondered if Maharene had volunteered to have her ears pierced or if Mose Baxter's people had insisted.

The applause started slowly but grew to a noise level that made the woman back up a few steps. Mose reached for her arm and pulled her toward the microphone. He whispered something in her ear and she smiled, showing gleaming-white teeth. Mose handed her the microphone and left her alone on the stage.

The crowd, recognizing that this living miracle was going to speak to them, silenced.

"Good ev-en-ing," she said, pronouncing each syllable in deep, warm tones. "I feel like Cin-da-rel-la stond-ing before you to-night. When the doctor on the Mercy ship said I could be cured forever, I did not believe him. I was a sad, ugly woman who only wanted to stay alive. Miracles are not for people like me, I thought. But I let the doctor give me the medicine. The next day, I could swallow easier and I thought this was good enough. Being able to breathe and swallow -- these things were good. In the past, the Mercy ship doctors cut the tumors away and tried to make me look okay. This time, there were no knives. There were no bandages. They put me in a room with another woman who took the Cure. The room had no mirrors. Every day for a week, we watched each other change without seeing how our own bodies were changing. The other woman's tumors disappeared! I felt my face and knew that mine were also going away. Together, we praised God, Who was turning us from monsters into people again.

"When I saw myself for the first time, I cried. After so many years of not looking like myself, I could no longer remember what I had looked like before. And now, I was pretty!"

The audience could contain itself no longer -- the burst of applause was deafening. Maharene's smile was wider and more beautiful than before.

Out of the corner of her eye, Evelyn saw Megan and the event organizer waving at her frantically. She nudged Julian, and they swept back onto the stage together, both clapping along with the audience. Julian gently pulled the microphone from Maharene's hand and Evelyn turned the girl toward stage right with a gentle arm around her shoulders.

"Wasn't that something, folks?"Julian said, wiping fake tears away. Evelyn had seen the routine too many times before to be impressed by his "sensitivity." She focused instead on the thin and shaking woman beside her.

"Missus B? It's you...I know you."

"Hush," Evie said. "Not here."

Julian continued with his patter as Evie led Maharene toward the door that would take them away from the stage.

Maharene stopped short of the door though. "You are so young! You were old, weren't you? Or was I so young that I was mistaken?"

"I'm not who you think I am."

"Where is Doctor B? He was so good to me. I want him to see that I am cured now."

"Please, Maharene, we need to get away from the stage," Evelyn whispered.

The door in front of them opened, and Mose Baxter appeared, silhouetted by the bright fluorescent lights behind him. "Maharene? I thought you would still be talking."

"Mister Mose, I know this woman from before, when I was sick! Is it not a miracle that she is here tonight?"

"Quite a miracle," Baxter agreed. "You're the hostess, aren't you? Thank you for the water earlier."

"You're welcome."

"How do you know Maharene?"

"She is the wife of one of my doctors," Maharene said loudly.

"I'm afraid she's mistaken," Evelyn whispered.

Baxter frowned. "Maharene, this woman is not who you think she is. I believe she's a local news anchor."

"No. She is the wife of Doctor B. She held my hand before and after three of my operations. She sang to me. Even if I did not know her face, I know her voice."

"It's just not possible, Maharene," Baxter said. "She can't be more than twenty-five...." His voice trailed off as he studied Evelyn's face. His eyes widened as realization dawned. "You're one of the trial patients."

Evelyn shook her head in denial, but knew she wasn't going to stem the tide. "I don't--"

"She is like me?" Maharene asked. "I thought Americans could not take the drug."

"It's not approved. But there have been medical trials here."

A roar of applause told Evelyn that Julian was done with the fundraising plea. "Let's get off the stage," she pleaded. "I can't talk about this here."

"But you should," Baxter argued. "You are a great example of how Promorterem can give people a second chance!"

"That's wonderful for people like Maharene...someone who never got their first chance. But Americans don't want to see their old people return to their youth. It's not accepted."

"Given the precipitous drop in fertility among Americans, you would think they would be more interested in something that keeps our best and brightest alive."

"That's not how people think, and you know it. They believe that a drug like this should only be given to those with the money to afford it."

"But it's cheap to produce! Why would I charge a fortune for something that costs only a dollar or two to make?"

"Because this is America, Mr. Baxter." Evelyn felt Julian's hand on the small of her back.

"Are you really standing here arguing with Mose Baxter?" he asked with a chuckle.

"Maharene, Mr. Baxter, this is Julian Harris, my husband."

"It's a pleasure to meet you," Baxter said, "even if you do look better in a tux than I ever will."

"The pleasure is mine. You, sir, are a bonafide genius. I just read the news into a camera; you transform lives."

"That's exactly what we were discussing here. Do you think Promorterem should be available everywhere?"

"Indeed I do. Just think of all the miserable deaths that could be avoided. Cancer, Lou Gehrig's disease, heart ailments...all of them wiped away with a simple injection! It's amazing."

"You know, of course, that the biggest objection is that old people -- people who have already lived long lives -- are suddenly young enough to compete in the job market. What do you think of that?"

"I say let 'em compete! Most of them probably wouldn't, anyway. Why should they? If they have the money for the treatment, they probably don't have to work."

"On the contrary...the treatment is cheap. Less than the cost of a cup of coffee."

"Really? Wow." He laughed. "Got a dose on ya? I'll buy it right now for twice that."

Baxter smiled and shook his head. "That's why we're looking at ways to regulate the drug that have nothing to do with money."

"For instance?" Evelyn asked, unable to contain her curiosity despite her urge to flee.

"Personal affidavits are one of the main methods we're considering."

Julian cocked his head to one side and squinted. "I don't get it."

"Basically, people will have to prove that they are valuable to society by getting vouchers from friends, family, and coworkers."

Julian smiled brightly. "In that case, my wife and I will live forever."

"Missus B already has a good start on that," Maharene said.

"Who's Missus B?" Julian asked.

"It's been wonderful to meet you both," Evelyn said hurriedly. "Have a wonderful night. Julian, we need to go or we'll miss our reservation." She gripped Julian's arm and turned him away from the billionaire philanthropist and his icon of success.

"What are you talking about?" Julian asked, looking over his shoulder. "We don't have reservations. And don't you think that was a little rude?"

"We're just the emcees, Julian. It would have been ruder for us to continue to monopolize them. Mr. Baxter and Maharene need to mingle with the donors."

Megan fell into step beside them as they marched toward the exit. "Everything okay?"

"Fine," Evelyn said through gritted teeth.

"This was quite a success. Years from now, this may be remembered as the first step toward Promorterem gaining acceptance in the United States."

"It's not the drug they have a problem with, Megan -- it's the people who have taken it."

"Not everyone can slip backwards in time as smoothly as you did."

Julian stopped short and looked at Megan, who was wearing a practiced expression of innocence. "What are you talking about?"

"Oh, no...is that still a secret after all this time? My lord, Julian...are you really so very dense?"

"What is she talking about, Evelyn?" Julian turned a hard stare on his wife, who closed her eyes as the tension and strain of hiding the truth drained away.

"I think she's referring to the fact that I am seventy years old."

Julian stepped backwards, away from both women. Evelyn could see his hands shaking, as if he had suddenly developed an advanced case of Parkinson's. "You can't be," he whispered. His head was shaking in time with his hands now. Evelyn began to worry that his head might shoot off his shoulders like a rocket at any moment.

"You think this is funny? You think I'm some kind of joke?" With each word he spoke, the volume of his voice increased. By the time he said the last word, the whole room had silenced and every head had swiveled toward them.

"Julian, now is not the time," Megan said warningly.

"It damned well is the time, you fucking bitch!" He pulled back his fist and slugged her.

Two hotel security guards who had been standing watch at the nearby door grabbed him from behind.

As Julian was dragged away, Evelyn turned toward Megan, physically trembling with rage even as relief swept through her. "What were you thinking?" she demanded.

"I was thinking," Megan answered in a calm, rational tone, "that you and I would be better off without him. He may be pretty, but he is way too difficult to work with. I found you both a great gig in Philadelphia, but he wasn't going to let you take it. Now, thanks to this scene, you and I will be moving onward and upward."

Evelyn shook her head in disbelief. "They're not going to want me now! You think Julian will keep my secret? That asshole will spread it around everywhere!"

"I'm counting on it."

Chapter 12 Philadelphia

"Good evening, Philadelphia. I'm Evelyn Bryant, and this is what you need to know today."

After a full year in Pennsylvania, Evelyn had to admit that Megan had been right. The station and the city embraced Evelyn and the new America she seemed to represent. Even as their search for a suitable co-anchor had floundered, the popularity of her news broadcast overshadowed that of all the other networks. After years of bantering co-anchors, the public seemed hungry for a simpler format featuring a single trustworthy face. That face happened to be Evelyn's.

Sure, the rumors flew that she had taken Promorterem. She never affirmed or denied them, choosing instead to say that no one should care about her personal life -- she was a news reader.

Megan was with her, of course. There was no denying that the two women were climbing the network ladder in tandem. And, together, they were headed for the summit: New York.

Evelyn's divorce from Julian had been, if not amicable, at least swift. News of his outburst put him on thin ice with the station. By the time Megan and Evelyn had settled into their new jobs, word came that he had been replaced by an older, more dignified newscaster and a youngish brunette with a picture-perfect smile. She heard -- through the media grapevine -- that he had found a featured reporter gig in Tucson, Arizona.

Evelyn had a small apartment downtown, close enough to the station that she could walk there even when it was snowing. On Megan's advice, she didn't buy a place to live -- Megan was sure they wouldn't be in Philly more than two years, tops. Evelyn didn't put much effort into decorating the place, either. A comfy couch, a quality bed, and a table with a couple of chairs was more than enough to fill the space. She hung exactly one picture: a photo from Africa that she had sent to Carmen years before. In it, she and Marty were surrounded by children who had come to the Mercy ship for help. In the upper right corner, Maharene's eyes stared solemnly at the camera.

#

"What a surprise," Mose Baxter said as he strolled into the convention hall. Maharene was by his side. She smiled thinly at Evelyn, who had been reviewing the words on the TelePrompTer set up for the Saving the Future Foundation event set to start with a little more than an hour.

"Hello, Mr. Baxter. Maharene."

"Missus B," she answered with a slight nod.

"I didn't think you'd still be involved with the charity, after what happened in Vegas."

"Well, like the old saying goes, what happens in Vegas, stays in Vegas." She gave them a half-smile. Neither of them returned the friendly expression. She cleared her throat. "I owe you both an apology. I never should have denied knowing Maharene."

"Does that mean you are ready to admit you are the Evelyn Mendoza who took part in the clinical trials in Oregon fifteen years ago?" Baxter asked. At her expression of surprise, he said, "You're right. Those records are confidential. But money can buy a lot of things. Peace of mind for Maharene, for instance."

"I'm not surprised that you know. After all, it's hardly a secret these days. Everyone thinks they know the truth about me. I am surprised you would tell me though."

"I thought you would want to know that your past has been safe with us."

"All those years off the grid in Africa -- I guess that's what has tripped all the investigators up."

"That and using your maiden name in the clinical trial. Whose idea was that?"

"My sister Carmen's. She had heard the rumors that Promorterem was returning people to their youth. She thought it would be better if I had a name I could use that would be clean of my history if it worked."

He nodded thoughtfully. "Impressive. Your sister is a bright woman. Your maiden name leads to all sorts of information you would probably prefer stayed in the past."

"Was," Evelyn corrected. "She died last week."

"I'm sorry to hear that."

"She would still be alive if the FDA would get off its bureaucratic ass and legitamize Promorterem."

"They have," Baxter said. "Just today, in fact. I'm going to be announcing it tonight. I'm sorry it's too late to help your sister."

Evelyn stared at him, her mouth gaping open slightly. The speech she had prepared -- her official coming-out party -- was now irrelevant.

"Are you all right, Missus?" Maharene asked, abandoning her expression of disinterest and coming to Evelyn's side.

"I'm just...speechless." She laughed weakly at her pun as the other two watched her with guarded concern.

Mose guided a chair behind her as Maharene lowered her into it.

"How...?" Evelyn asked.

"They just ran out of excuses. It was bound to happen eventually."

"How much will it cost? Will anyone be able to afford it?"

He smiled. "I own the technology and the patent. I've set the price at ten Affidavits of Value for one dose. In order to get Promorterem, you must have ten people who think you are worth saving."

"That won't be hard."

"Probably not," he said with a shrug, "but it will force people to speak face to face. An affidavit must be obtained with a digital information recorder that requires a drop of blood, a retinal scan, and a voice imprint delivered within a few minutes of each other."

"So your plan is to send sick people out into the world with these devices and have them beg for affidavits?"

"Most people won't have to beg. Their friends and family will save them. Remember, we're only talking about ten people."

"I don't have ten people I could ask."

Maharene laughed. "You are on the television. You would have a hundred volunteers to save you. People like Mose will die long before you."

#

"We have an offer from L.A.," Megan said.

Evelyn looked up from her tablet and caught Megan's eyes in the mirror. "Really?"

"Yeah. I don't know about you, but I've trudged through enough snow in my life," she said with a smile.

"What about your fiance?" Evelyn asked.

She shrugged. "Either he comes or he doesn't. He knows my career is my priority."

Though they had never been more than reluctant allies, Evelyn still felt the urge to counsel the woman. "Are you sure you want to do that? I think he really loves you. You might not have a chance like this again."

Megan laughed. "Your thinking is so old-fashioned! I guess Promorterem doesn't update old programming, does it? This is just my first lifetime, Evelyn. I still have at least a thousand years ahead of me. We all do. I can fall in love and do the family thing in a hundred years. Hell, three hundred years from now!"

"What if you don't find another man like him?"

"There are thousands of men like him. There's only one L.A."

A month later, when Evelyn and Megan left Phillie, Megan wasn't wearing her engagement ring anymore.

Chapter 13 California -- 2105

The mansion, a huge pink monstrosity in what used to be the fame capital of the world, seemed mildly neglected. Stepping out of her pink hovermobile, Evelyn noted that her car blended into the facade. She found it somewhat ironic that Mose Baxter had chosen to live in a city abandoned decades earlier by the very people who once made it interesting. She was sure the billionaire had gotten the place for millions less than its previous owner had paid.

While the instant communication of the early twenty-first century began the California exodus, the invention of personal hovercrafts with automated controls had made it completely unnecessary for film stars to live close to the studios that produced their films. Baxter, along with a fair number of geeks from Silicon Valley, snapped up the Beverly Hills properties at bargain prices. The place plummeted from style icon to a city of desperately lonely introverts within the space of a decade.

Evelyn walked up the stairs and rang the doorbell.

A moment later, a beautiful black woman with silver hair answered the door. Her warm eyes flashed and hardened and her mouth pulled down into an angry frown.

"Hello, Maharene. May I come in?"

# # #

Evelyn was surprised that there were no servants; she knew that Mose Baxter's widow had plenty of money. Nevertheless, the home was as silent as a library after closing time. She felt the undeniable urge to whisper for fear of disturbing the ghosts that surely haunted this place.

Maharene's voice broke the silence. "Why are you here?" Her accent was softened slightly by her years in America, but she still had a tone as clear as a ringing bell.

"I'm dying, Maharene."

"Again?" She arched a doubtful eyebrow at her. "You can't be more than five years from your last dose."

"Closer to ten."

"Where were you last year, when Mose lay dying in my bed upstairs?"

"I was sure you wouldn't need my help. After all, Mose--"

"Was shunned by you stupid Americans. He created the thing that gave the world eternal life, and for that, he was treated like a pariah. No one would give him a voucher. No one! He only needed one more. He could still be here, if you had only come to our door then."

"You didn't call me."

"But you knew. You reported the story on your news show."

"No! I didn't. That woman isn't me...hasn't been me for years now."

Maharene narrowed her eyes. A moment later, she reached into her pocket and withdrew a pair of glasses. She peered at me through them before leaning back in her throne-like white-and-gold chair. "That changes nothing. You still knew that he was sick."

"I didn't realize how sick he was. I didn't know that he couldn't get the ten affidavits he needed."

"I predicted this. I told you once that you would outlive him. And so you have." She clenched her jaw and scanned the room for several seconds. "You are lucky, Missus. I still remember how you held my hand when I was just a scared child. You gave me the comfort and love of a mother, even if it was only for a little while every few years. I will do as Jesus taught: I will give you what I wish you would give me." She held out her hand.

"You don't owe me anything, Maharene. I don't even know if I want to go on, and I don't think I can get ten anyway."

She nodded. "You are no longer on the television. It will be harder for you...and that is right. But I will not deny you my affidavit. I will not have you curse my name on your deathbed. Give me your device."

Evelyn opened her bag and removed the device. She stood and walked it over to her erstwhile friend.

"My name is Maharene Baxter. Evelyn Bryant should live."

#

After the affidavit was complete, the two women had nothing left to say to one another. Evelyn left the younger, yet older, woman in her shabby mansion and flew to her small apartment on Mission Bay in San Diego.

She had bought the place back when she was on television. At the time, beachfront property was still expensive. Of course, with scientists predicting that the San Andreas Fault would soon shake everything west of it into the ocean and the rising level of the oceans already encroaching on the beaches, prices were dropping precipitously. If she had a mortgage on the place, she would already be figuratively underwater, if not literally.

The place felt unfamiliar, even though it looked exactly as she had left it a few days before. The Mid-Twentieth-Century replica furniture seemed wrong -- too much rattan maybe, or not enough leather. It looked -- suddenly -- like an old woman's apartment. She laughed, realizing that she may have been fooling herself, but she certainly wasn't fooling anyone else. She was an old woman, no matter what the facade of her body claimed. She had outlived her time.

Nearly a week of searching and she had only three affidavits to show for her efforts. Sure, her granddaughter promised a fourth, but only if she could last through the summer. The way Evelyn felt at that moment, she doubted she would make it through June. She sank into the sofa that faced the condo's best feature: a picture window with a view of the bay. A few sailboards skimmed the water in the distance, but the beach itself was empty. San Diego was still a little too cold at this time of the year.

Maybe, she thought, death isn't such a bad thing. She hadn't been afraid of death the first time she had cancer. More than sixty years ago now. Not long after Marty...she still missed him. Maybe death would mean a reunion. What if he was waiting--

A knock at the door pulled her from her reverie. Evelyn pushed herself up, feeling the weight of her years, to answer it.

"Hello. Are you Evelyn Bryant?" asked the young man on the other side of the threshold.

"Who is asking?"

"My name is Tim Carver, and I think you may be my great great grandmother."

# # #

She knew why she invited him in, and it had nothing to do with his striking resemblance to Desmond or the fact that he seemed nice. No, those definitely weren't the reasons she let the tall young man into her small space. Instead, her greedy soul grasped at the possibility of a new, untapped source for affidavits -- those few words and that insignificant drop of blood that would allow her to stay alive.

"May I get you anything to drink?" she asked solicitously after she guided her guest to the most comfortable seat in the house. "Tea? Coffee? Water?"

"Um...no, thank you. I don't want to take up more of your time than necessary. I'm not even sure you're the right Evelyn Bryant. You see, my great grandmother, Barbara Bryant-Reese, assumed that my great great grandmother had died years ago. The last she heard from my Evelyn was that she had terminal cancer."

"Around 2045 or so?"

He blinked before meeting her eyes. "Yes," he answered slowly, "but I couldn't find a death certificate."

"I was one of the first Americans to receive Promorterem. Through a clinical trial."

"Is it true? Are you really my great great grandmother?" He teared up.

"I don't know. If our only connection is through Barbara, I'm afraid I'm just a step relation. But you look remarkably like my son."

"Desmond Shaw was my great grandfather."

She did her best to look distraught. "How could he have not told me?" She buried her face in her hands.

"He didn't know. My great grandmother never told him. And neither did either of my aunts."

"I don't follow."

"My grandfather had two cousins who were also half-siblings. They were all born around the same time in 2034."

Evelyn lost her breath.

"That's when you married Dr. Martin Bryant, right?"

She nodded.

"Only Barbara is still alive. Her sisters are gone, and, of course, Desmond and his family were killed in London." He glanced around uncomfortably. "The story she told me...well, it's a little racy."

"Nothing you could possibly say would embarrass me, son."

He shrugged before spitting three sentences out in one breath: "She says they used Desmond like a party favor for a week. They all wanted to punish their father for marrying you. And they all wanted babies."

"Then why didn't they tell us?"

"You went on your honeymoon and didn't come home until the children were half grown. By then, all three of the sisters had realized their anger at their father had been misdirected. And, of course, two of them had married and had more children. They planned to tell you that you had more grandchildren, but they never got around to it."

"How did you find me?"

"I was helping my younger sister with a genealogy project and we couldn't find your death certificate. Now, a hundred years ago if you couldn't find a death certificate, you would just assume the person was dead and the certificate was lost in the bureaucracy. But with medical advances..."

"You thought I might still be alive."

He nodded.

"Thank you for finding me."

"I really only did it to satisfy my curiosity," he said. "I don't want to turn your life upside down."

A bitter laugh escaped her lips.

"I mean, you're a television star. I didn't come here to mess that up for you."

"I haven't been on television for a few years."

"But I've seen you--"

"Not me," she said abruptly. "The network bought my name and replaced me with a cheaper version. Besides, I keep getting cancer -- over and over again."

"Because of the Promorterem?"

"No, of course not. I'm just genetically predisposed. This is how my story will end: cancer wins."

He shook his head. "Just get another dose of Promorterem."

"I need ten affidavits to do that."

"Yeah? So?"

"I don't have ten people who care if I'm alive or dead."

He stood up and walked to the plate-glass window that looked out over the beach. "You've lived more than a hundred years and you don't have ten people you can turn to? What kind of life have you lived?"

She swallowed down an indignant retort. Smiling apologetically, she said, "I've done the best I could. Before today, I had only a daughter and a granddaughter to call family. I haven't been on television for a while now. I never had a lot of friends. Marty Bryant was the love of my life. I miss him. I wouldn't let people get close to me for a long time because I was afraid of getting hurt again." After a moment, she wondered aloud, "Maybe Marty is waiting for me."

"There is nothing after this, Evelyn. Science won. If you want eternal life, you take Promorterem. That's all there is to it." He spotted her affidavit collector on the kitchen counter where she had laid it when she arrived home. As Evelyn watched, he walked toward it with a purposeful stride. "Three? You've only got three affidavits so far? When did you find out you were sick?"

"Less than a week ago. But I've only got a few more people I can ask. I don't have the money for any black-market affidavits."

"So you're giving up?"

She nodded. "That's why I came home."

"I can give you one."

"Don't. Three people have already wasted affidavits on me. Save yours for someone you love."

"I could love you."

She smiled and shook her head. "You know what I thought when you showed up at my door saying I was your long-lost relative? Do you? My very first thought was 'I'm saved.' Not 'How wonderful' or 'That's amazing.' No. My first thought was of myself. If Marty is somewhere in the heavens waiting for me, he won't recognize me. That's what

Promorterem has done to us. It hasn't made us better people -- it's made us into a world full of grovelers. We make friends for what they might be able to do for us in the future. We join groups as a form of insurance against death. People used to become involved in causes because it made them feel better. They made friends because they felt an affinity with the other person. Friendship used to be part of a fulfilling life. Now, it's just a tool for extending it." She walked to where her descendent stood and took the device out of his hands. "If you really want to help me, don't give me an affidavit. Give me your word that you will stay more interested in living your life than extending it."

Chapter 14 Megan

Los Angeles was all blue skies and green plants -- everything Philadelphia wasn't, especially in January. Evelyn couldn't get comfortable in the city though. After a weekend trip to San Diego, she decided that the southern city was a better fit for her. She found a place on Mission Bay and bought it with her signing bonus from *Good Day, L.A.*

For all her bluster about her career coming first, Megan was clearly upset that her former fiance refused to leave Pennsylvania. For the first time in the nearly fifteen years since they first met, Evelyn felt sorry for the woman. Megan's looks were fading -- she was, after all, past forty-five. She went to the doctor for the slightest ache or pain, each time hoping that some fatal disease was invading her body.

As the months rolled by, Evelyn watched as her ally grew decidedly paler despite the bright sunshine of their new hometown. Megan stopped smiling and seemed to be tense most of the time. Evelyn could remember a time -- now long past -- when she would have rejoiced to see the woman suffer. But years of proximity had dulled her harsher impulses.

"Are you all right?" Evelyn asked one Friday when Megan looked particularly forlorn.

"I'm...lonely, that's all. Don't worry."

"If we don't worry about each other, who will worry about us?" Evelyn asked with a crooked smile.

Megan looked up and smiled back at her. "I suppose you're right. How are you adjusting to California?"

Evelyn shrugged. "A studio is a studio. Doesn't much matter if we're in Los Angeles or New York."

"But what about your downtime? I heard you bought a place in San Diego."

"I did. It's good. Quiet. I imagine the summer will have a different vibe, but so far, it's very relaxing."

"I'd like to see it sometime."

"Are you busy this weekend? You could catch the train with me."

"Seriously?"

"Yeah. I have an extra bedroom. You're more than welcome."

She seemed to consider it, but then shook her head. "No. I should stay here. I have a date tonight, anyway."

"Maybe next weekend."

"Maybe."

Evelyn walked to the couch where she and her co-host -- currently a young man named Ed -- sat every weekday morning. She pulled out her tablet and began reviewing the day's schedule.

A meek woman who served as the program's producer approached her and cleared her throat.

"Yes, Willa, what is it?"

"Did you forget to go to makeup?"

"No, I didn't forget."

"Oh." Willa stared at her for another minute as if she were trying to formulate a sentence.

"Speak, Willa," she barked. The girl gave her the creeps.

"I'm sorry to bother you, but you don't look right under the lights."

"What do you mean?"

"You look...yellow."

Evelyn left her tablet on the couch and walked to the nearest mirror. She had only seen jaundice in other people -- the patients who came to the Mercy ship -- but she knew what to look for. She curled her tongue back and saw that the area beneath it was almost fluorescent.

"What's wrong?" Willa asked.

Evelyn met her eyes in the mirror. "I'm sick."

"You've got to be kidding me," Megan said, appearing behind her left shoulder in the mirror. "And just when you were starting to wrinkle. Of all the dumb luck!"

The cancer was back, and this time it was attacking her liver. Once the diagnosis was made, the doctor handed her an affidavit collector and showed her how it worked. It was small -- about the size of a cellphone -- with a series of sharp needles concealed along one side of the device. The needles didn't pop out until an affidavit was given. The doctor asked Megan if she would give Evelyn an affidavit and Megan agreed. She walked Megan through the procedure, demonstrating the device to both of them. "When you have ten affidavits, return here and I'll administer the Promorterem."

"Do I need to make an appointment?" Evelyn asked.

"No. It's just a quick injection. But then, you know that, don't you?"

She looked warily at the doctor. "Why would you think that?"

"Oh, please. You're Evelyn Bryant. Everyone knows you were one of the trial patients."

"Everyone?"

"Well...everyone in the medical field does. You're the success story!"

"Those trials were supposed to be anonymous."

"Oh, they were. But everyone knows that you're Patient E in the research published about Promorterem."

The two women left the office and walked to the elevator in silence. Once inside the silent box, Evelyn asked, "Did you know about that?"

"Yes."

"Why didn't you tell me?"

"Why does it matter? You are Evelyn Bryant. Patient E is just part of who you used to be."

"Is that how you discovered my secret?"

"It played into it." The elevator opened and they walked out into the bright, white-marble foyer of the building. "I cancelled my date," Megan said.

"You didn't have to do that. I'll be fine."

"I know you will, but San Diego sounded better than another lame weekend in L.A."

"Where am I going to get nine more affidavits?"

"Don't be ridiculous. You are already beloved by Angelinos. You could get nine affidavits walking to my car."

"Isn't the idea that we're supposed to have nine family members or friends who care enough about us to want us alive?"

"Maybe for regular mortals, but not for people like you."

"Why would strangers give me affidavits? I'm just a face on a screen. What if they give me one and then someone they really love gets sick?"

"There are no takesy-backseys, Evelyn." Megan took her by the arm and dragged her out onto the sidewalk. Approaching the first person they saw, she said, "Excuse me...do you know who this is?"

The woman, middle-aged and plump, looked annoyed at first, but when she focused on Evelyn's face, she exclaimed, "It's you! *Good Day, L.A.!*"

"Yes, this is Evelyn Bryant," Megan confirmed when Evelyn didn't answer. "If you knew that this woman were sick, would you give her an affidavit?"

"You mean for Promorterem?"

"Exactly. Would you?"

"Of course! She's such a nice person."

"You don't know that," Evelyn said quietly.

"Of course, I do," the woman said, taking her hand in a grandmotherly fashion. "I see how you talk to people every day. You are so sweet to them. You make everyone feel at ease."

"I've only been here a few months."

"You're the only news hostess I trust." She frowned as she looked at the building the three of them were stopped in front of. "This is a medical building, isn't it?"

Megan nodded. "We've just been to see a doctor. Evelyn has cancer."

Before Evelyn had a chance to object, the stranger had her affidavit collector and was recording her affirmation of Evelyn's significance.

# # #

On the train to San Diego that evening, Evelyn noticed for the first time how many of her fellow commuters recognized her. Normally, she kept her head down, her attention focused firmly on whatever book, magazine, or television show she was currently interested in. Megan, however, refused to let her hide behind her tablet. Instead, she insisted that they speak -- rather loudly -- about her diagnosis. At first, she tried to shush her, but it seemed that Megan's strategy was working. Before they stepped off the train in San Diego, Evelyn had the other eight affidavits she needed.

"See?" Megan asked rhetorically. "No muss, no fuss. That's what a famous face will get you."

Evelyn shook her head and laughed in disbelief. "That won't work forever, you know."

"Maybe not," she answered with a shrug, "but it works for now."

As they walked to Evelyn's vehicle, the only sound between them was the rhythmic click of their heels on the concrete.

"Are you hungry?" Evelyn asked after starting the hovercraft.

"Don't you want to go to a clinic first?"

"Why? I won't die over the weekend."

"Maybe not, but I'd prefer not to spend the next two days looking at your yellow face."

"Fine." Using the onboard computer system, she found the nearest clinic and directed the vehicle to go there. "After this, will you want to get some food?"

"Do you have anything at home? I'm not really in the mood to be in a restaurant."

"Canned chicken. Maybe some pasta. Not much else."

"If you have some sauce too, I can work with that."

"Probably. If not, we can always order in."

"I like the way you're thinking now," Megan purred.

Evelyn had a sudden vision of the direction this night was headed in. It wasn't what she had thought at all. "Listen, Megan..."

Megan put a hand on top of Evelyn's. "No. Don't say anything yet. Don't forget, I know what you did for a living once upon a time. I've seen the footage...I know you enjoyed yourself. I'm not looking for anything permanent. Just a little relaxation."

"But I'm just not interested--"

"Is it me?" The expression on her face was pure devastation. "I used to be so beautiful! Men fell at my feet, Evie...you know what that's like!" Tears welled in her eyes. "No one has looked at me with anything but sympathy since we got here! I'm not looking for forever. I just want to feel someone's hands on me--"

Evelyn leaned forward, putting a hand on either side of her face. "Stop. You're still beautiful. You could go back to

Philadelphia tomorrow and I bet your ex-fiance would take you back."

Megan met her eyes and smiled. "You look like a Muppet. Go get your Promorterem."

Megan turned out to be a decent chef, considering the limited ingredients available in Evelyn's kitchen. The vaguely Italian dinner filled the empty spot both of the women had by the time it was ready to eat. They sat on the sofa that faced the beach and chewed silently, each of them mulling over the day in their own way.

Megan spoke first. "You look better already."

"It takes a few days to get the full effect."

"You'll probably look a decade younger by Monday."

"I suppose so." Evelyn glanced at Megan's dish, which was nearly empty. "May I take your plate?"

Megan lifted it up and Evelyn reached for it. Megan didn't release it right away; instead, she held it tightly, forcing Evelyn to look at her. "Why won't you?"

"It's a sin." She pulled harder, and the plate slid from Megan's grasp.

"More of a sin than the ones you have already committed? You slept with Julian for years before you married him."

"Why do you want me so much? You don't even like me. How would having sex with me change that?"

"Why do you think I don't like you?" She smiled as if Evelyn had told a joke. "I admire you! I always have. You're an amazing woman. You're brave, brilliant, beautiful...you walked away from everything you knew for a chance to start over."

Evelyn shook her head. "You don't understand. I only did what I had to do under the circumstances. And then you exploited my secret!"

184

"I don't have any real talent, Evie. Never have. The only thing I can do is spot talent in other people and try to use it for my own gain."

Evelyn set the dishes in the sink and turned on the water, more to drown out Megan than to clean them. She counted to thirteen and took a deep breath. When she turned off the water, she held up a hand to keep Megan from talking. "Listen. What you did to me...almost ruined my second chance. I never wanted to marry again after I lost Marty."

Megan laughed disbelievingly. "So you turned back the clock -- gave yourself decades more life -- and planned to spend all those years alone?"

"I never wanted this," she answered, shaking her head sorrowfully.

"The martyr act would be more believable if you hadn't just been dosed with Promorterem."

"Twenty years ago, I wasn't afraid to die. I only joined the trial because my sister begged me to do so."

"No one forced you today."

"You're right. And I'm going to fight death kicking and screaming for as long as I can, because what I did...what I let the doctors do to me...it's the ultimate sin. If I believe in God...when I die, Megan, there's only one place I can go and it won't be Heaven."

"There's no such place. No heaven, no hell. That's all superstitious garbage." Megan unfolded herself from the couch and walked to the kitchen. She put her hand on the small of Evie's back, sending an electric current through her. "I'm forty-five years old, Evie. I've never been married to anyone or anything except my career. That means I'm married to you. I'm more devoted to you than anyone else in my life. I have spent the better part of fifteen years at your side. The least you can do is--"

Evelyn turned toward her and took her face between her palms. Pulling her forward, she touched her lips gently to Megan's. The velvet touch made her heart race and her body surge toward the fire kindled between them. Releasing her face, Evelyn slid her mouth to Megan's ear. She traced its shape with her tongue before whispering, "Just once. Just tonight."

Megan shivered under her touch before hungrily kissing Evelyn. "Just tonight," she answered in agreement as they melded together in a flash fire of passion.

Evelyn woke up sobbing.

Megan appeared, fully dressed, in the doorway, a coffee mug in her hand. "Are you all right?"

"Bad dream." She could still feel Marty's disappointed gaze on her skin. She could see the tribunal where she was convicted of licentiousness and sentenced to eternal damnation. She brushed her arms with her hands in an attempt to loosen the bonds of her subconscious. Damn Alan for filling her with this Christian morality. Why couldn't he have just left her alone?

"I made coffee. Get dressed. I thought you might show me the town."

"Thanks. I'll be out in a few."

Megan pulled the door closed and Evelyn stepped out of bed and walked to the full-length mirror that hung on her closet door. Already, she could see the signs of Promorterem. Her skin was tighter around her midriff and the tiny lines at the corners of her mouth were gone. The nanos seemed to be working faster than they did the first time she took the Cure. She wondered if it was because there was less work for them to do or if scientists had refined them even more for faster results.

Opening the closet, she pulled out a soft blue t-shirt and an ivory cardigan. From her bureau, she removed a pair of straight legged jeans. Once dressed, she looked in the mirror again and pulled her hair into a ponytail and decided to skip the makeup.

She opened the door and the scent of freshly brewed coffee wafted toward her. Megan was sitting on the sofa that faced the picture window, her back to Evelyn. "This is an amazing view to wake up to every morning," she said without turning around. "I understand why you commute."

"With the trains, it's so easy and fast. I would never have been able to do this fifty years ago, but now I don't understand why more people aren't living outside of L.A." Evelyn picked up the cup of coffee Megan brewed for her and added some sugar to it. She stirred the liquid slowly, staring at the back of her -- what was Megan now? She wasn't a friend...she never had been a friend. A life companion? A lover?

"What's wrong?" Megan was looking at her. "You look...weird."

"I'm not weird. I'm just thinking."

"Don't think too much."

"What are we now?"

"You're the talent and I'm the agent. Just like it's always been."

"But last night?"

Megan shrugged and turned back to the view. After a few moments, she said, "I think I slept better here than I have slept since we left Las Vegas. I wonder what it is about the air here?"

"I think it's a little cooler here than in L.A."

"Maybe that's it. Or maybe I just like the smell of ocean air."

Chapter 15 2105

Evelyn's thoughts drifted back to Megan, now several years in her grave. Promorterem was never an option for her.

"Are you all right, Evelyn?" Zeta asked from behind the kitchen counter. "You're so quiet tonight."

"Why would you want to hear my stories? I'm just an old woman who has spent too many years on this planet."

"So, the moroseness is age related, huh? I always thought it had more to do with the knowledge of impending death."

Evie turned and looked at her great-great-granddaughter with pursed lips.

"But you don't have to die!" she said with exasperation. "How many times do Tim and I have to tell you that? We can get you enough affidavits to keep you alive."

"In your lifetime, how many people have you seen die?"

"Both of my aunts are dead."

"But those were sudden deaths, right? Nothing could have saved them? And you weren't present..."

Zeta broke eye contact with her ancestor. "I wasn't around when Aunt Alicia died, but I saw Aunt Bella fall."

"Fall?"

"She tripped at the top of a landing. When she reached the bottom, she was gone."

"I knew she must have died in an accident but...she fell down some stairs?"

"Yes. The irony was that she had just taken the Cure a month before. She looked beautiful -- and as young as I am now. The Cure is amazing, you know? That's why I don't understand why--"

"Because I don't want to break my neck on a flight of stairs," Evelyn answered, cutting her off. "No one dies of natural causes these days."

"It must be decades since anyone has."

Evelyn sighed and shook her head. "That's not true. People die of natural causes every day -- just no one you know."

"But you just said--"

"I was exaggerating...as old people are wont to do," she said, a smile too tired for her youthful face flitting across it.

"Have you known anyone?"

"I was just thinking about the last person I knew who died from something other than an accident. Her name was Megan Richards."

"Who was she?"

Evelyn smiled. "That's a very good question. I knew her for forty years, and I'm still not sure I know."

Chapter 16 Megan and Jordan

Megan never mentioned their night together to Evie again, but, strangely enough, the two women became friends for the first time in their long history. The L.A. gig stretched on; for a while, Evelyn believed she would work the West Coast morning show forever. She started her twenties over again, while Megan reached and passed fifty without any signs of illness.

The morning of the London terrorist attack, Evelyn reported on the deaths of five thousand people in her concerned but remote tone. It was a gas attack -- a deadly compound released in every underground station in and around London during the afternoon rush hour. Three thousand died from the gas; another two thousand died in the panic that ensued.

Megan held off the official notification until Evelyn was off the air. As soon as the cameras were cleared, she took her friend by the hand and led her away from the crew and into a small room, where she handed her a cell phone and said, "Hit send."

After a few moments, a male British voice said, "Good evening, Miss Bryant. I've been awaiting your call."

"Who is this?"

"My name is Detective-Inspector Smythe, and I'm very sorry to inform you that your son, Desmond Shaw, and his family were victims..."

The phone fell away from her ear and she didn't hear the words that followed. She didn't need to. Her eyes searched the room, seeking something to latch onto, something to keep her from drowning. When they finally found Megan, Evelyn said, "Take me home."

Megan wrapped a strong arm around her and led her out of the building.

When she awoke the next day, she couldn't remember how she got back to San Diego.

Then she realized that she wasn't home. The photographs on the dresser all featured famous people standing next to Megan: the politician who was almost elected president; the businessman who actually won; the movie star who was nominated for a dozen Academy Awards; a prominent writer; and, of course, Jordan Meriweather, the long-dead Las Vegas newswoman. That one raised a bitter taste in the back of her throat. She closed her eyes against the infiltration of bad memories -- things that were better left in Vegas.

A soft rap at the bedroom door prompted her to roll over. "Come in," she said, her voice scratchy and raw.

The door opened about a foot and Megan appeared. "I wasn't sure if you were awake yet."

"Just now, actually."

"Would you like some hot tea? That should soothe your throat." She retreated from the bedroom.

After a moment, Evelyn stood and followed her into the living area of the apartment. It was small and bland, with furniture in neutral shades. "Why am I here?"

"I couldn't get you on the train in the state you were in last night. Too many prying eyes."

"Was I crying?"

"Wailing, actually. I don't think I've ever heard anything like it before. And you weren't exactly using your words."

She felt the muscles in her jaw go slack and remembered what had made her catatonic the night before. "My son is dead." She let the words float from her mouth and hang in the air. She tried to weigh them in her mind -- to see if they were true or just something awful from a bad dream. Slowly, the words sank and engraved themselves on the floor at her feet -- true, real, and unchangeable.

"I'm so sorry," Megan said softly, and Evelyn believed her. "I've never lost anyone like that. I mean, so suddenly."

"What about Jordan?" Evelyn asked. "You two were close, weren't you?"

She inhaled sharply. "I meant a relative. Jordan was really just a work colleague."

"I thought you were closer than that. After all, you spent time together away from the station."

She shrugged and shook her head dismissively. "Not much."

"Really? I just assumed you were Ronnie's Aunt Megan."

Megan stiffened for a moment and seemed to forget how to breathe. When she regained control of her muscles she turned wary eyes on Evelyn and pulled a knife from the butcher block. "How would you know that?"

Evelyn backed up. "Just something Ronnie said once."

"How did you even know Ronnie?"

Evelyn realized Megan's stiffness wasn't dissipating and her fingers were turning white around the knife's handle. She answered slowly. "Jordan. When I first came to Vegas, she kindly took me to lunch with Ronnie and her."

Megan's head was shaking back and forth in small, almost imperceptible increments. "I should have known," she said softly. "I should have seen."

"What are you talking about?"

Megan glared at her with a ferociousness Evelyn hadn't seen in years. "Don't play dumb. You know. You've probably suspected for years, but...now you know!"

The pieces of information she had collected for twenty years clicked into place as if they were pulled together by magnets. "You...killed Jordan? But why?"

"She was supposed to be my ticket out of Vegas. Let's face it -- Vegas is a backwater compared to L.A. or New York. Hell, even Phoenix is a bigger market!" Her aggression seemed to drain out of her and she fell back against the counter for support. "I sold Jordan to New York."

Evelyn wrinkled her nose in disdain. "You can't sell a person."

Megan shook her head with exasperation. "You know what I mean. I shopped her profile and resume around every major market I could find. I figured she wouldn't be able to resist a chance at the desk of a major news outlet. I knew she wanted out of Vegas and away from her ex. I just didn't count on Ronnie spoiling it."

"So? you could have shopped Jordan again after Ronnie was out of the house. She was already seventeen, right? This is the job Jordan passed on because Ronnie didn't want to leave her boyfriend?"

Megan nodded in confirmation. "But by the time Ronnie was out of the house, Jordan would have been past forty. I wouldn't have been able to get anyone to even take a look at her package -- and Jordan wouldn't have fought for it! We'd talked about getting out of Vegas...starting over in a new city and conquering it. If Jordan had taken Crista Andres' position, I was set to move into national corporate management! No more small-town bullshit -- I'd have been working directly for the network."

"But she turned down the job."

Megan stared at her. "And, then, there you were: young, beautiful, and so full of poise and ease that I thought you were just acting. That's why I dug into your background:

you didn't seem real. And, as it turned out, you weren't. What's it like being sixty in a twenty-year-old's body, Evie? For that matter, what's it like being eighty and young?"

"It's not as great as you would think."

"Can't be that bad," she scoffed. "Look at me...the age is really starting to show, isn't it? I'm older than Jordan was when..."

"You pushed her?" Evelyn supplied.

Megan looked away from her. "It wasn't like that. I was arguing with her. I had gone to her to suggest that she move to a less-visible position."

"She was the most popular anchorwoman in Vegas!" Evelyn said, incredulous.

"The public's memory is short, especially in a place like that. People don't live there forever...they stay a few years and move on. Which is what I intended to do. Besides, being the lead anchor of the morning show would have been a good fit for her. The position required much more interaction with the public, more chances to mingle with the watchers, more interviews that would have allowed people to see her personality...it would have been perfect for her."

"But she didn't agree."

"It was an accident, Evelyn, I swear."

"How did you get out of the building without them knowing you were there?"

"I had a key."

"You were more than friends."

Megan met her eyes. "We had a special connection."

"Why are you telling me all this?"

"You knew! I could see it in your face as soon as you walked out of the bedroom!"

"I didn't. I had no idea."

Megan slid to the floor; the knife's blade scraped against the ceramic tile. "Then why do I feel so much better?"

"Because guilt is ridiculously heavy." Evelyn reached down and took the knife from Megan's limp hand. She lowered herself to the ground next to her dazed companion. "The only way to feel fully free is to turn yourself in."

"For a suicide?"Megan laughed. "I bet they won't even believe me."

"Ronnie will."

Her head dropped and she stared at her hands. "I can't."

"Yes, you can. You have to."

"But I'll never get my do-over! I haven't even taken a single dose of Promorterem."

"You're right. You won't get to be young again. You won't have children. But you could still find a husband and be happy."

"Who would want someone who is guaranteed to die on them in thirty years?"

"You don't know that for certain. You may live twice as long as that."

"I don't want to live to death, Evelyn."

"Everyone dies. No one is permanently immune."

"Evelyn, sweetheart," Quinella said with her sickly sweet voice and treacly smile. "Come in! Come in! We were just speaking about you."

Evelyn glanced around the room full of network suits. Ever since the Los Angeles morning show had gone national, she had found herself feeling more and more like a diver in a metal cage surrounded by sharks pretending not to notice the tasty morsel in their midst. Today, she wondered if the cage had finally rusted away. With Megan gone -- she had died only a few weeks before -- no one in the room was on her side. Even as Megan had begun her long slow fade into oblivion, she had remained by Evelyn's side in negotiations.

Quinella was young -- not Promorterem young, but an actual person born within the last half of the twenty-first century. She was also privileged to be the daughter of the CEO of the network, which was why she found herself in the boardroom on the thirty-fifth floor instead of in a cubicle several floors below. She had been raised to believe that beauty grew from the inside out, but had learned that an attractive exterior could hide interior ugliness. In the few years that Evelyn had been forced to deal with her, she had come to believe that no seedling of beauty was waiting to burst forth from Quinella; instead, the child was a walking, talking weed.

Evelyn gritted her teeth and walked toward the lead negotiator without hesitation. "Quinella. It's a pleasure to see you again."

"The pleasure is all mine, I'm sure," she answered, smoothing her red-silk skirt instead of extending a courteous hand. "Have a seat, darling."

Evelyn's stomach knotted, but she sat where she was told.

"I can hardly believe it's already been two years. *Tempus fugit*, no?"

Evelyn laughed politely, as did the rest of the suits.

"So, Evelyn, we've got a special offer for you today. I'm sure it will come as no surprise to you that you have one of the most recognizable and trusted names in journalism today. Evelyn Bryant has come to mean as much as Walter Cronkite, Barbara Walters, or Crista Andres to the average viewer. Most of them turn to your show as the leading source of what is happening in our world today."

"That's very flattering, but--"

"Oh, I'm not saying this to flatter you. As everyone in this room will confirm, this is the absolute truth. We have vetted the audience feedback thoroughly. We have done countless consumer research panels on this very subject. Your name is so valuable that we, as a corporation, would like to buy it from you."

"You want to buy my name?" Evelyn felt her eyes crinkle in confusion; she willed herself to slip into her smooth mask of composure. "How would that even work?"

"It's actually to your benefit. You, as an individual, don't really have the resources to protect your own image. After all, the courts have repeatedly ruled that individuals may not copyright their own names, because the chance of overlap is too high. However, the network can trademark it and apply pressure to others who may or may not have been born with the same name."

"So you would bully anyone who was unfortunate enough to have been named Evelyn Bryant."

Quinella smiled. "It wouldn't be bullying. We would merely apply pressure to convince them that continuing to identify themselves as Evelyn Bryant was more trouble that it was worth."

"But what good is my name without my face?"

"We're not getting rid of your face, Evelyn. In fact, you should see this offer as a guarantee of future employment! Why would we invest millions in a name that we intend to discard?"

"Millions?" Evelyn's paycheck was big -- in the six-figure range -- but it hadn't topped a million in the past.

"Of course. We're prepared to offer you twenty-million dollars for the exclusive and eternal rights to your name." Quinella's shoulders rose slowly as she leaned forward. "It's almost like we're paying you to promise to stay with the network for the rest of your life."

"What if I want to leave at some point in the future?"

"You could always revert to your maiden name. And you would still have a nice little nest egg to live on -- no reason at all to seek a new position in the news business."

Evelyn's heart ached at the thought of ever parting with Marty's name. "I can't do it."

Quinella sat up straight and looked around the room. The various yes-men stopped muttering. A few cleared their throats. "I suppose," Quinella mused aloud, "we could offer you an exception on the name. Have you grandfathered in, so to speak."

"But there must be others already out there with the same name."

"You'd be surprised how many people will part with their name for a little cash."

Evelyn looked down at her hands on the polished antique wooden table. Twenty million was more money than she would ever need. That, plus her annual salary, would guarantee her comfort for the rest of her life. She couldn't see a downside. "Okay."

Chapter 17 San Diego, California -- 2105

Zeta stared at the picture of Megan and Jordan. It was the one thing Evelyn had taken from Megan's apartment after she died. "Jordan was beautiful," she commented.

"I always thought so."

"Megan, though...she wasn't pretty."

Evelyn smiled. "She was an acquired taste. I admired her for her strength of will and formidable personality."

"But she never would have been on-air talent," Zeta probed.

"No. Her features were too sharp. And her smile rarely reached her eyes."

"Did she turn herself in?"

Evelyn nodded. "Eventually. I promised to keep her secret, but she said that me knowing made it that much harder for her to keep her own confidence."

"What happened to her?"

"She was sentenced to live to death."

Zeta shuddered next to her. "I can't believe they ever did that."

"People thought it was the humane way to deal with criminals."

"Was she locked up?"

"Actually, she was deemed unlikely to reoffend. They just inserted the virus into her body and sent her back into the world."

"She must have been terrified...knowing that if she were ever sick, the Promorterem would kill her instead of heal her."

"I don't know...I think she accepted it pretty well. In a lot of ways, I think her punishment freed her. She spent so many years hoping for a terminal illness that would allow her to start over. The realization that this was the only life she was getting changed her outlook. She swallowed her pride and called the man who had wanted to marry her back in Pennsylvania."

"She lived happily ever after?" Zeta asked with a half-smile.

"Not exactly. He had moved on. It had been years since we'd left. But at least she talked to him. She worked out a list of things that she wanted to do before she died, and she started doing those things. She went sky-diving, she tried puffer fish, she took a trip to outer space on the space elevator--"

"In other words, she was suicidal."

Evelyn laughed. "I suppose that's one way to look at it. But these were all things she wanted to do but didn't because Promorterem can't save you from accidental death."

"When did she die?"

"About seven years ago now. She was seventy-nine. She never married, but she had one hell of a good thirty years."

"Do you think living to death was fair?"

"Zeta, sweetheart, I think Promorterem is the real punishment."

#

"How is she?" Tim asked quietly as he came through the door.

"She seems fine," his sister answered in a similarly low voice.

"I'm dying, not deaf," Evelyn called from the sofa. In the last few weeks, she had found herself watching the people on the beach even more than usual. "Why don't you ask me how I'm doing."

"I'm sorry, Evelyn. You're right. How are you?"

"I'm comfortable enough. Zeta's taken good care of me." She turned to look at her great-great-grandson. "You know, I have more than enough money to go to a care home."

Tim shook his head. "We want to spend as much time with you as we can, since you won't agree to take the Cure. Besides, I did a little research. Your pain from this cancer shouldn't be bad. We'll be able to treat you with over-the-counter painkillers right up until the end."

"You children shouldn't have to see that -- death up close isn't pretty."

"From everything I've read, people used to die at home all the time -- all the way into this century, as a matter of fact. It was rare, though. By the end of the twentieth century, most people died in hospitals or care homes."

"I don't need the history lesson, Tim. I lived through it more than once. It's not as easy as you think, seeing a loved one die."

"I never said it was easy. You can still change your mind, Evelyn. You have half of the affidavits you need already. I can get you the other half today, if you want."

She reached up and ran her hand along her descendent's jawline. "It's funny the features that persist. Your profile is remarkably like Desmond's. And Zeta has my eyes, I think."

He sighed, but he didn't fight her changing the subject. "I've found photos of other family members. Your parents, I think. Your mother was gorgeous."

"She had a strong streak of Spanish in her -- pale skin, light eyes, dark hair. She was striking."

"And you look a lot like her."

201

Evelyn smiled. "I was the lucky sister. Carmen looked the most like my father. Her features were heavy compared to mine."

"What about Karen?"

Evelyn shook her head, remembering the sister who had taken her own life. "She was pretty, but also very smart. She and Carmen got all the brains, my father used to say. But I did all right for myself, I think."

"You outlived them both."

"That's not proof of intelligence, Tim. Just luck...or a lack thereof." She took a deep breath and closed her eyes as she exhaled. "Tell me: what have you been up to?"

"I went to Phoenix."

She opened her eyes and cut them sharply at Tim. "Why?"

"I wanted to meet your daughter."

"How did that go?"

"I didn't think she was going to let me in, at first. She didn't believe I was who I claimed."

"What convinced her?"

"I knew where you and Marty got married, and I knew that Desmond went to the wedding."

"What did she have to say?"

"Nothing nice, as I'm sure you would suspect."

Evelyn looked straight ahead, noticing a young-looking couple strolling together in swimsuits that seemed too modest for their toned bodies. She imagined that they were one of the lucky couples who survived the Cure -- two people so devoted to each other's soul that they could overlook their partner's failing body until Promorterem was an option for the one who got sick last. She liked to think that she and Marty would have been like that: able to weather the hurricane that the Cure produced. "Her father rescued me from a bad situation. I mistook my feelings of gratitude for love."

"You don't need to explain," Zeta said.

"No, I think I do. If anyone deserves an explanation, it's you."

"Zeta's right, Evelyn. It doesn't matter why you left Alan Shaw. The fact of the matter is we wouldn't be here if you hadn't."

"How old am I now? I've received so many do-overs that I can hardly remember my original birthdate."

"You're nearly one-hundred-and-fifteen years old."

"The Promorterem…I think it alters the brain just a little bit every time it rebuilds it. Maybe it makes guesses instead of repairs when it comes to memories."

"Why? What do you think has changed?"

"Everything."

About the Author

Susan Wells Bennett is a native of Arizona, which is why Arizona is always a character in her books. Whether she is writing heartbreaking loss, humor, exploring advancing age, or advancing technology, she brings every story to life in under an unforgiving sun, breathtaking desert vistas and resort style metropolises. The reality of her conflicts, loyalties and resolutions are a hallmark of her works, regardless of the genre in which she is currently working.

If you have enjoyed this exploration of the morality of buying immortality, consider her other titles, all available through Inknbeans Press and other fine booksellers:

Circle City Blues
The Prophet's Wives
Thief of Todays and Tomorrows
An Unassigned Life
Forsaking the Garden
Wild Life
Charmed Life
Night Life
New Life
Just One Note
A Fallow Season

More From Inknbeans Press

Emjae Edwards, *You'll Wake Up One Morning*
Annarita Guarnieri, *The Importance of Being Shine*
Jim Burkett, *Shadows of Bataan*
Candy Ann Little, *Murder of an Oil Heiress*
Rusty Coats, *Out of Touch*
Kitty Sutton, *Mysteries From the Trail of Tears*
Dawn Hood, *Pray and Bring Chocolate*
David Rowinski, *The Book of Complements*
Dorothy Legge, *Poems of Faith and Love*
Denise Kennedy: *I Wish I Were*
R. H. Ramsey: *Like Shards of Glass*
Perle Butcher Lyon, *Rebel Wife*
Kristann Monaghan: *The Running Experiment 2*
Eric Pullin, *The Magical Tree*
Hugh Ashton, *Without My Boswell*
Hugh Ashton and Andy Boerger, *Sherlock Ferret and the Poisoned Pond*
Andy Boerger: *Letting Go*
Jt Sather, *How to Survive When the Bottom Drops Out*
Virginia Czaja, *Get Real*
Jackie Williams, *Baby Steps*
Liam McCaughey, *Collected Werks*
Pico Triano, *Let Sleeping Dogs Lie*
Ey Wade, *When Clouds Touch*
Robin Bee Owens, *The Wand*
Michael Gryboski: *The Man With Ruby Eyes*
Jackson Horvat -*The Vortex Entrance*
Adrian Comanschi – *Duke of Norlandia*

www.ingramcontent.com/pod-product-compliance
Lightning Source LLC
Chambersburg PA
CBHW060437180626
46817CB00007B/2854